The Wooden-Shoe People

by Lloyd C. Hackl

An Illustrated History of the
First Swedish Settlement in Minnesota

The story of the real Karl Oskar and Kristina

"Better wood in the shoes than in the head."

F.M. Eckman, May 1904

ISBN 0-934860-53-X

Published by Minnesota Treasures
Center City, Minnesota

Distributed by
Adventure Publications, Inc.
P.O. Box 269
Cambridge, Minnesota 55008

Copyright © 1986, 1990 by Lloyd C. Hackl
2nd Edition

Design by Theresa R. Nordby
Printed by Sentinel Printing, St. Cloud

All rights reserved under International and Pan-American Copyright Conventions. No part of this book may be produced in any form or by any means, electronic or mechanical, including photocopying, without permission in writing from the author.

Outsiders called the immigrants the wooden-shoe people because they wore their handmade shoes when they worked in the fields

Acknowledgments

The Chisago Lakes area is blessed with a number of historians. Of special help have been Ted Norelius and Carl Henrikson, Jr. of Lindstrom. Emeroy Johnson's pioneering work on Erik Norelius is important to any study of Swedes in Minnesota. Sue Team, a great-great grandaughter of Per and Carin Anderson, who lives in Carlsbad, California, graciously supplied family records and some photos. Dale Fredell and Lorens Johnson of Center City shared their photographic collections. Friends Will and Karen Kitchen of Cambridge worked several years ago with me on two projects relating to early Chisago County. Randolph Johnson kindly showed me relevant historic sites in Cambridge. Many local residents such as Lillian Porter and Paul and Carol Norelius shared stories and family records. The new Chisago County Historical Society research center at the Lindstrom library made scanning of early local newspapers convenient. The research facilities of the state historical society in St. Paul provided access to early state and local records. Valuable, too, were the archives of the Chisago Lake Evangelical Swedish Lutheran church in Center City. Special thanks are due to my wife, Barbara Paetznick, who read the manuscript and to Cyndi, Debbie, Isadora, Dr. Henry Watson and Antonio. Finally, thanks are owed to the state of Minnesota and the Community College system for providing me with time to complete the project.

May 1986

Gunnar Torhamn's mural in the Hassela church depicts important figures in the parish's history. In the lower right is Per Andersson with his hand on the shoulder or Erik Norelius. Photo by Karl Akerholm.

TABLE OF CONTENTS

The Wooden-Shoe People

Introduction 1
Early Arrivals 3
Founders: the Real Karl Oskar 9
    Crossing 12
    Settlement 16
    Moving On 19
In Their Own Words: Memoirs and Documents 21
Center City: from the Farm Center to Resort Area
    Upper Town 52
    Lower Town 61
    Resort Era 68
A Selected Bibliography 74

GUIDEBOOK

A Walking Tour of
Turn-of-the-Century Center City 7
Auto/Biking Tours of Historic Sites
in Southern Chisago County 84
Following the Moberg Trail 93

Introduction

The future must have seemed promising that bright Sunday afternoon in Sweden when the hundred or so members of the Andersson party stepped from their ancestral soil to the wooden planks of the sailing ship that was to carry them to America. None had been more than a few miles from home before. What little space was left in their America trunks was filled with precious seeds for planting in the virgin soil of a country they knew about only through letters and shipping company advertisements. Their real-life journey and the subsequent settlement they founded in remote Minnesota Territory, which became legendary in the fictionalizing of their emigration by Swedish novelist Vilhelm Moberg, is the subject of this book.

When the Andersson party arrived at their destination, outsiders called the immigrants the wooden-shoe people because they wore their handmade shoes when they worked in the fields. In the spring of 1851 they settled in a heavily wooded area along the shores of a big lake called Ki-chi-saga by the Indians who sometimes camped on its banks. From the pine and hardwood forest the wooden-shoe people built log cabins; from basswood trees they fashioned tools, furniture and shoes. In the clearings they planted crops. For the first few years everything raised was needed for survival. In many ways their lives in the new land didn't seem much better than the ones they had left behind in Sweden.

CENTER CITY

Shortly after moving to Center City a few years ago, I reread Moberg's epic about the lives of a Swedish emigrant family headed by Karl Oskar and Kristina Nilsson who had settled in Minnesota Territory. In the last section of his final book, *The Last Letter Home*, I found myself once again in the farm home of the aging, widowed Karl Oskar as he carefully unfolded the Swedish map of Ljuder parish and traced with a gnarled finger his childhood path to Kristina's home; later, visiting her Chisago Lake lakeside gravesite, he leaned his crippled body against the homemade wooden marker to straighten it. Moved again by the passage, I put the book down without finishing and bicycled along the lakeshore past the old church to the cemetery

A family poses for a final picture together in the old country. For emigrants in the mid-nineteenth century, it was often the last image of home or loved ones they would have.

east of town where so many of the real-life people Moberg based his story on lie beneath the chalk-white stones. It is a journey I have since made many times.

Overgrown by the advancing grass, some of the earliest stones have begun to disappear. Their fading epitaphs, carved in Swedish and rubbed almost smooth by more than a century of harsh Minnesota winter winds, grudgingly yield up familiar sounding surnames in an increasingly unfamiliar language. By the end of the nineteenth century, names like Svensson had been Americanized to Swanson, Nilsson to Nelson, Bengston to Benson and so on. During parts of the years 1948-50, Moberg had stayed in the Chisago Lake area researching his novels. Ted Norelius, a retired, long-time editor of the *Chisago County Press* and grandson of Erik Norelius who left Sweden with the first party in 1850, remembers that the Swedish author often went into local cemeteries late at night with a bottle and a flashlight to read the tombstone script. Many Chisago County pioneer names made their way from these gravestones to Moberg's printed pages.

MOBERG

It was Moberg's stories that first drew me to the town, Center City, that the real-life Karl Oskars helped build. Over the past ten years I have analyzed volumes of historical materials and talked to and corresponded with many descendents of the early settlers of the colony; the result of those investigations is this illustrated account of the Swedish settlement. In many ways this effort has been the unraveling of a mystery. Often people said that they were sure that their particular ancestor was the real Karl Oskar. Karl Oskar, of course, is a fictional character, but readers will discover that there is among the early settlers of Chisago County a man who may well have been the inspiration if not the model for the hero of Moberg's novels.

This book tries to capture for the first time in one volume, often in rare photographs, the story of the first Swedish settlement in Minnesota. I hope the reader will find the story of the Swedish people who first came to Ki-chi-saga as compelling as I found it to be.

Provided here, also, are both a walking tour of the town and a biking/driving map of sites in the immediate area surrounding Center City. This guidebook section should aid visitors who may choose to walk, bike, or drive to sites referred to in the text. For readers unable to visit southern Chisago County, the photographs, maps, and descriptions provide a good picture of the land the wooden-shoe people claimed in 1851 and the town they founded.

A gravestone in the abandoned pioneer cemetery on the south shore of the lake. Erik Norelius' mother had followed her emigrating sons as far as the churchyard in Sweden so that she could say she had followed her sons to the grave. She did not think she'd ever see them again, but within three years she found herself and her family sailing to America where they settled for a short time near Little Lake in the Center City Colony.

An Ojibway family in front of their home near Balsam Lake, Wisconsin. They are descendents of people who often camped on the shores of Chisago (North Center) Lake and traded with the settlers.

3   Early Arrivals

Early Arrivals

Who were the first settlers in the Chisago Lakes area? Little is known about prehistoric inhabitants, perhaps because few excavations have been made, but evidence from these suggest that it has been settled for at least several thousand years.

According to most historians, the first white man in the St. Croix Valley was Greysolon du Luth who, with a party of five Canadians, visited the area in 1680. The seventeenth and eighteenth centuries brought invasions of fur trappers and traders who nearly wiped out the beaver in the valley.

In more recent times, Ojibway migrating from the eastern United States had moved the resident Sioux out of the Chisago Lakes area by the mid-nineteenth century. Bloody battles were fought early between the two tribes, one at the Dalles area near the present interstate bridge at Taylors Falls which, for a long time afterwards, was referred to by the Indians as the "Valley of Bones." By the 1840's only a few scattered skirmishes between the two tribes occasionally reminded the early lumbermen residents of their presence. When the first Swedish immigrants arrived in the 1850's only small bands of Ojibway remained, some camped around the shore of the big lake, and a few others living several miles north of the present site of Center City who operated a maple sugar camp. These few survivors soon migrated to reservations in western Wisconsin. Remnants of these lost tribes can be found near Danbury and Balsam Lake.

Little remains in Center City of these early native Americans: part of a burial mound alongside Highway 8 in town, arrowheads and tool fragments turned up occasionally by farmers' plows, and a few items such as bartered, beaded bags handed down through generations of farmers. The white settlers who replaced the Sioux and Ojibway changed everything, even the place names they found. Ki-chi-saga, the Ojibway word for the big lake (meaning large and beautiful), became Chisaga and finally Chisago in 1851, the last change owing to a typographical error at the state legislature at the time the county was established. The name Ojibway itself was soon corrupted by the white man to Chippewa.

A large influx of white men accompanied the signing of a treaty in 1837 in which the Ojibway and Sioux ceded to the U.S. all land westward to the Mississippi. Drawn by reports of the extensive pine

Wannigans, floating houses, followed the loggers, providing them with a place to eat—and sometimes to sleep—during the log drive downstream.

Loggers setting up camp. Many of the Center City settlers worked in the pineries to the north during the winter months to supplement their incomes.

A camp sawmill where logs were rough-cut for the trip down river.

The three logging photos in this section were taken by Carl Henrikson, Jr. and are of a later logging drive.

A logjam at Taylor Falls. The June 26, 1884 Taylors Falls Journal *reported "Another of those large log jams formed in the dalles at this place Sunday morning, filling the river for a long distance above the bridge. Driving crews were put to work immediately, and on Tuesday the boom company's pile driver was engaged in pulling out logs. The first big haul was made on Wednesday, and was witnessed by hundreds of people. When the logs moved in a body, which generally occurs several times before the jam is removed, it is one of the grandest sights ever witnessed. The roaring and grinding, snapping in two of large logs, and shouts of hundreds of voices, combine to make it an event never to be forgotten."*

forests in the upper St. Croix region, loggers followed the river and its tributaries upstream into the pineries of East-Central Minnesota and Wisconsin even before the treaty was ratified a year later. Before long the woods echoed with the ring of axes and the whine of sawmills, and the spring rivers were soon filled, sometimes clogged, with the winter's cuttings as they floated downstream on the St. Croix River to the sawmill site at Marine Mills.

According to the *Minnesota Democrat* newspaper of April 22, 1851, Erik U. Norberg, a Swede, was in the Falls of the St. Croix area the summer of 1850. When he arrived at Big Lake, as present-day North Center Lake was then known, a Yankee hermit by the name of John S. Van Renssalaer already lived on an island in a cabin reportedly well stocked with books. With the coming of the Swedes, Van Renssalaer packed up his books and moved north about twelve miles to the unsettled Sunrise area.

Some maintain that three Swedes, Oscar Roos, Carl Fernstrom and August Sandahl, who in October of 1850 built a cabin near the present village of Scandia, were the first Swedes in the area. But Norberg also spent the fall and winter of 1850-51 in the Center City vicinity, living in a dugout covered with branches and bark. He may have preceded the Scandia trio or, possibly, even ridden upstream on the same boat with them. The Scandia men left their Hay Lake cabin in 1851, the same year that a Swedish party led by Per Andersson arrived in Taylors Falls to found the permanent colony at Center City.

Almost four decades before the Andersson party reached the Chisago Lakes area, the Swede Jacob Fahlstrom had been in the Ft. Snelling region; later he farmed in Valley Creek and delivered mail to the Falls of the St. Croix settlers in the 1840's. Fahlstrom is generally assumed to have been the first Swede in Minnesota. Born on April 25, 1793, he came to North America with an expedition led by the Earl of Selkirk, but was separated from the group in the Hudson Bay region. Helped by Indians along the way he worked his way south, arriving in Minnesota sometime in the 1803-05 period. For twenty years he lived the life of a voyageur and fur trader for the Hudson Bay Company. In 1823 he married Margaret Bongo, an Ojibway, at Fond du Lac. He served thereafter as an agent for the American Fur Company for two years at Leech Lake, at Sandy Lake in 1826, and at Mille Lacs in 1827 before the family moved to Ft. Snelling where they lived for the next twenty years. In 1840 Fahlstrom moved to Lakeland in the St. Croix Valley, finally settling in Valley Creek. During this latter period

Erik Norberg

Fahlstrom

7 Early Arrivals

Fahlstrom carried mail between Prairie du Chien and the settlement at the Falls of the St. Croix.

On one occasion while carrying mail upstream, Fahlstrom stopped to fraternize with the Ojibway, an event which did not escape the notice of their foes, the Sioux at Kaposia, who captured him on his way back downstream. Threatened with his life, Fahlstrom was, after some time, able to talk his way free.

According to newspaper accounts, it was with great delight that Fahlstrom visited the Swedish colony at Center City in the 1850's to hear his native language spoken. He also traveled often to St. Paul to hear sermons delivered in his native Swedish.

Fahlstrom died in Valley Creek in 1859 where he is buried with his wife.

So who was first among the Swedes? That question sparks lively debate among local historians to this day. Did Norberg arrive before, after, or with the Roos group? Wasn't Fahlstrom even earlier? And what about George Nelson, a trapper who in 1842 worked the St. Croix River, or Nils Tornell who was murdered in the Falls area in 1848? Perhaps the question will never be answered to everyone's satisfaction, but there can be no disagreement that the first permanent Swedish settlement in Minnesota was at Center City.

Part of the tapestry in the Chisago Lake Lutheran Church which portrays the history of the Swedish settlement at Center City.

Hassela, Sweden where Per Andersson and many of his party began their journey to America is located in a lake setting not unlike the land area they chose to settle in Minnesota.

A Chronology of Events Which Shaped the Early Swedish Settlement of the St. Croix Valley

1823   Ft. Snelling completed at the confluence of the Minnesota and Mississippi rivers. It was the center about which the first Minnesota settlements revolved. Earliest settlers came from the Assiniboin colony in Canada founded by the Earl of Selkirk in 1811. Jacob Fahlstrom, the first Swede reported in Minnesota, came to America with the Selkirk expedition.

1837   Treaty: Ojibway and Sioux cede all lands between the St. Croix and Mississippi rivers to the white man. Ratified in 1838, the treaty opened up Minnesota to settlement. Ma-ghe-ga-bo, a spokesman for the Ojibway, said at the signing "We wish to hold on to that which gives us life—the streams and lakes where we fish, and the trees from which we make sugar." Governor Dodge agreed to their request.

1838   First steamboats come to the Falls of the St. Croix.

1839   First sawmill in territory built on the banks of the St. Croix River, at Marine Mills, giving impetus to a huge logging business.

1842   Begun six years earlier, the sawmill finally begins operating at St. Croix Falls.

1848   Area around Ki-chi-saga surveyed. First land sales made at land office in St. Croix Falls, which was then a part of Washington County. Speculators from the east were thwarted by local squatters who carried clubs to the land auctions and intimidated them.

1849   Minnesota Territory established. Land office moved to Stillwater.

1851   Chisago becomes a county. Swedish colony founded at Big Lake (present North Center Lake). Facing no competition for land from the outside, the Swedes are content to squat on their land. None actually buy land until 1853; they pay $1.25 an acre.

1853   Road from Stillwater to Taylors Falls completed. Stage run opened.

1854   Cholera epidemic. Some in colony are victims of the disease. One boat traveling from Stillwater to Taylors Falls stops enroute to discharge an ailing family of Swedish immigrants who are left to bury their dead in shallow graves on the river bank. Survivors are later rescued by members of the Center City colony.

1856   First bridge across the river at Taylors Falls.

1857   The so-called "Cornstalk War" near Sunrise. The "war" concerned a group of thirty light cavalrymen from St. Paul chasing five frightened braves through a cornfield. One brave and one soldier were killed. The matter was considered a farce.

1857   National economic panic.

1858   Minnesota becomes a state.

1861   Civil War begins. Many Swedes serve, including two of Per Andersson's sons; the oldest, Andrew, dies of pneumonia at Ft. Snelling.

1862   Sioux Uprising in Minnesota River Valley, far to the west and south of the Center City colony. Nevertheless, the colony builds breastworks on two isthmuses. A cannon is brought to the settlement from Ft. Snelling. No hostile action occurs near the colony.

1865   Civil War ends. Large influx of Swedish immigrants to area continues through the 1880's.

The bark Odin on which the Andersson party sailed in 1850.

Founders: the Real Karl Oskar

The Crossing:

On August 17, 1850 more than one hundred farmers from northern Sweden boarded the bark Odin in the Swedish port of Gavle to begin an eleven week voyage to America. Leader of the party was Joris Pelle (Per) Andersson from Hassela parish in Helsingland. Richest of his neighbors, Andersson's generosity made it possible for some of the party to make the journey.

According to the diary of Erik Norelius, who at 17 was one of the youngest emigrants, the party had intended to stay together to form a colony in America, but by the time the group reached Moline, Illinois where they wintered, only half remained. Nine had died during the crossing, one as the Odin entered New York harbor on October 31. From New York the party had sailed upriver to Albany, then ridden the immigrant train to Buffalo, and proceeded on the Lake Steamer Sultana westward across Lakes Erie, Huron and Michigan to Chicago where they disembarked on November 14.

Up the Illinois River they went by canal boat to Peru, Illinois. From that point, some on foot, others by hired wagon, they headed for the Swedish colony at Andover. They arrived in Andover on the 23rd of November in the midst of a severe snowstorm. Instead of the bustling, prosperous town they'd expected to find, they discovered only small houses scattered across the landscape. There was not even enough shelter for all the newcomers.

It was a short trip from Andover to Moline where Per Andersson and his family spent the winter with Jon Olson, who'd earlier led a group from Sweden to America. Also staying that winter with Olson was Per Berg and his family who'd emigrated with Olson's party.

Sometime during that winter Andersson exchanged letters with another Swede, Erik U. Norberg, who was staying in the Taylors Falls, Minnesota area. Norberg, dissatisfied with the Bishop Hill colony in Illinois where he had been living, had traveled to Taylors Falls in 1850 and reportedly spent the fall and winter in what was to be later known as the Chisago Lakes area. The spot on the peninsula where he dug a hole and protected himself from the winter with branches and bark drawn over the opening was for years after called Norbergsholmen and is the site of the present city of Center City.

Erik Norberg, the Swede whose letters drew the Andersson party to the Chisago Lakes area. Bishop Hill Assn Collection.

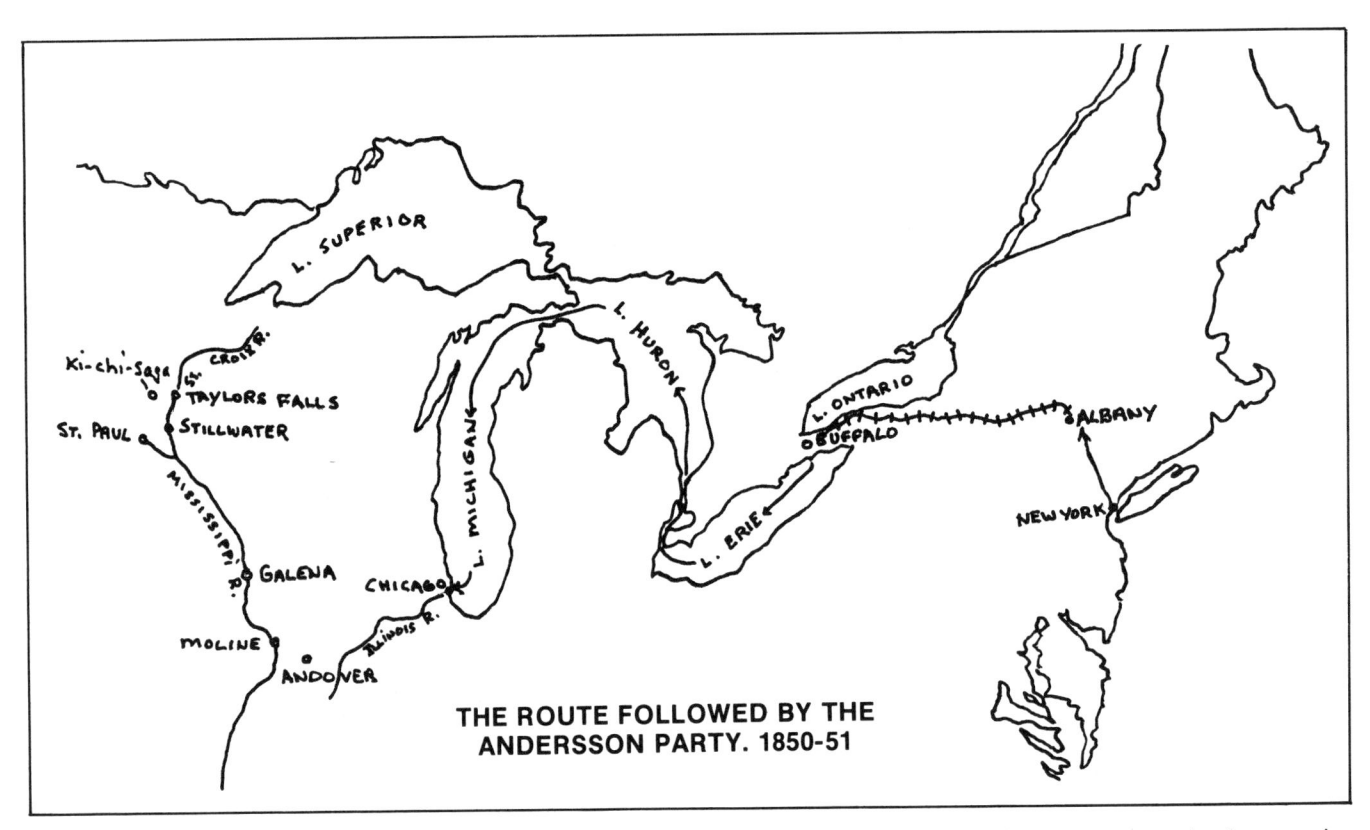

THE ROUTE FOLLOWED BY THE ANDERSSON PARTY. 1850-51

The journey of the Andersson party from Sweden to Minnesota Territory. Moberg's fictional Karl Oskar Nilsson and his party followed the same route, even traveling in America on ships of the same name.

During the winter of 1850-51 Norberg wrote to Andersson in Moline, extolling the wonders of the lakes area in the Minnesota Territory and including a map. Norberg's description of the hunting and fishing prospects must have been irresistible to Andersson, who was not an enthusiastic farmer, for when the ice on the Mississippi broke up in spring he headed north with his family and his hired hand, Daniel Rattig. Also accompanying him were Per Berg and Peter Viklund and their families. Another Swedish family, that of Anders Svensson, joined the party in Galena. Svensson had arrived in the midwest by a different route than the main Andersson party, traveling by water from Sweden to New Orleans and from there up the Mississippi to St. Louis. St. Louis had been a disastrous experience for the family. Someone ran off with their money and the entire family was ill with cholera, a child and a newborn succumbing to the disease. To their good fortune they were given $50 by the touring Swedish singer Jenny Lind who happened to be in that city. The money

13 Founders

enabled them to proceed Northward to the Swedish settlements in Illinois.

From Galena, the Andersson party headed north first on the Mississippi, then on the St. Croix River, by steamship. They disembarked at Stillwater, a thriving lumber town in Minnesota Territory. There existed at this time only a few thousand people in the entire Territory with major settlements at St. Paul and Stillwater.

Proceeding upriver from Stillwater on watercraft, very likely either the *NOMINEE* or the *YANKEE*, the party arrived at the hamlet of Taylors Falls on April 23, 1851 where Norberg awaited them. Only a few stores and small houses made up the hillside hamlet of Taylors Falls that spring. The inhabitants were almost exclusively lumbermen who operated the sawmill at the falls of the St. Croix. After finding temporary lodging for the women and children, Norberg led the men ten miles westward through the hardwood forests and swamps to the shores of Ki-chi-saga, the "Big Lake", cutting a trail over which the others could later travel. This last stage of the journey took nine days.

SWEDISH PASSENGER ARRIVALS—1850

Per Andersson — age 33 — Hassela, Helsingland
wife Carin — 36
son Anders — 12
son Daniel — 8
dtr Helena — 4
dtr Ingrid — 2

Daniel Pehrsson Bill — 19 — Hassela, Helsingland
(Rättig)

Per Berg — 49 — Hög
wife Martha — 46
son Nils — 19
    Twins
dtr Karen — 19

Peter Vikland — 26 — Angermanland
wife Christina

Anders Swensson — 43 — Ostergotland
wife Cajsa Lisa — 34
son John F. — 12
dtr Johanna Charlotta

Founders 14

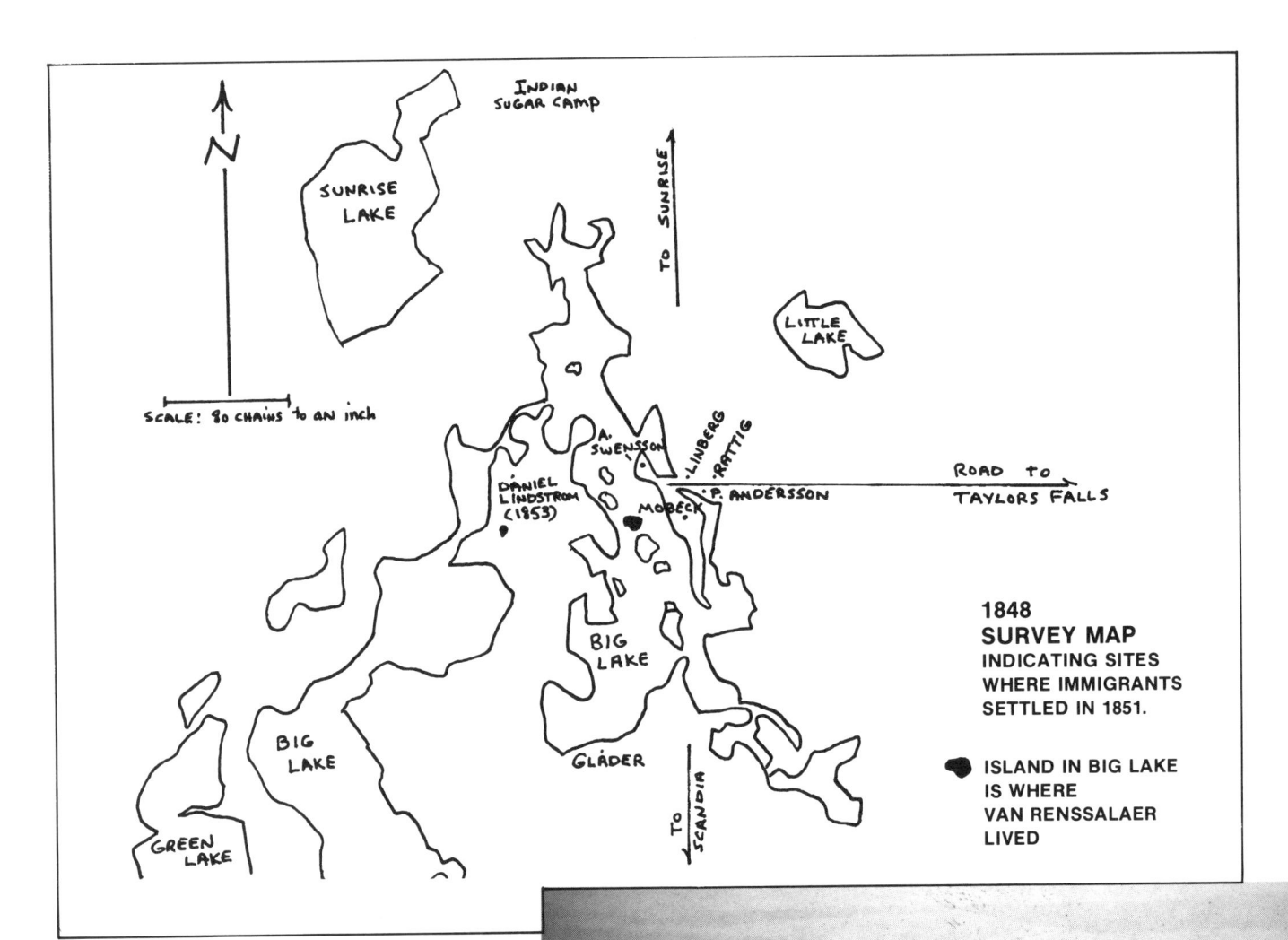

Land bought by the first settlers in 1853-54.

Clearing the land. Circa 1880.

15 Founders

The journey of the Andersson party as chronicled by Erik Norelius was almost identical to that traveled by Moberg's fictional counterparts: both parties numbered initially about 100, nine died on the trip across the Atlantic, and the route followed from New York to Taylors Falls was the same, right down to the name of the lake steamer, SULTANA.

Settlement:

The first months at Big Lake were spent clearing land, planting oats, potatoes, rutabagas and wheat, and building a log cabin. Hunting and fishing provided additional food. The entire party of sixteen lived that first summer and fall in the single log house that was constructed.

Other, later, settlements in the Minnesota Territory were not always as fortunate; in some instances only the kindness of the Indians, who supplied settlers with venison, made early survival possible. Not so with these Swedes. For the first years, the members of the Andersson party "cut their coat according to their cloth;" that is, they raised everything necessary for their survival. Only Per Andersson owned a horse, and later a team of oxen, which was shared by all in clearing land. But no one in the settlement had much money and there was no credit in Taylors Falls or Stillwater, some 27 miles to the south. Having no money meant that the heavy bags of seed and flour had to

Hemlandet, a newspaper edited by Erik Norelius, gave immigrants news from the homeland.

An early steamboat on the river near Taylors Falls. Passengers and freight reached the Falls either by steamboat or stage until the coming of the railroad.

be carried from those two sites on one's back until Andersson got his oxen. Having no money for nails meant that wooden pegs had to be carved from the surrounding hardwoods in order to hold house and furniture together. In the fields almost all wore the traditional wooden shoes which earned them the nickname of the "wooden-shoe people" among the non-Swedes. Because it remained ethnically pure, within a short time the settlement was referred to by outsiders as "Swede Lake".

Beginning with the winter of 1852-1853 Andersson, his hired man Rattig, and others were able to earn money during the winter months by working in the pineries along the Snake River some sixty miles to the northwest.

In 1854 Erik Norelius, who had stayed behind in Illinois and Ohio to further his schooling as a minister, arrived to hold religious services and teach school during the summer; a road had been cut between Stillwater and Taylors Falls enabling him to travel that distance by stage. By the time Norelius arrived, the Baptists had already held a camp meeting at the lake. In fact, Erik's brother Andrew, who'd arrived in the colony in 1853 with his parents, later moved to Isanti County where he served as Baptist preacher for many years.

Axel Carlson's drawing of Per Berg's haymow where the first Lutheran indoor church services were held. The spot where the Haymow stood is marked with a monument at the northeast end of the cemetery.

Per Berg's haymow served as a site for the first indoor services in the predominantly Lutheran colony. The first public structure built later was a school house which was also used for church services. Many lively debates took place on Sundays when missionaries traveling in the area turned up. When the lay preacher for the day, originally either Andersson or A. P. Dahlhjelm, had finished his sermon, a visiting preacher would stand up and deliver yet another one, inviting churchgoers to accept his creed and dogmas as alternatives to those they'd previously heard. The colony was to remain, however, staunchly Lutheran. In 1854 the Lutheran congregation was officially formed and in 1855 received their first ordained pastor, Erland Carlsson.

Anders Svensson had the town platted in 1857. His house was built on the peninsula where Norberg had spent the winter of 1850-51. The only "hotel" in the settlement for years, the Svensson house was located east of the present courthouse. One of the founders of the Chisago Lake Lutheran congregation, Svensson was excommunicated in 1856 when he became a Methodist. He later provided land for the Methodist church in Center City, a structure built in 1858 which still stands on the southeast corner of Main and First in Upper Town. Late in the century the Methodist congregation moved to neighboring Lindstrom.

Four cemeteries had early been established in various parts of the settlement, farmers in each area hoping that locating the cemetery near them would attract the building of the church nearby. After

Erik Norelius' pulpit in his Vasa church. The pulpit is designed to look like an open Bible, creating the effect that the preacher is speaking stright from the word of God. Members of the Andersson party were pietists, "awakened" individuals who, in the eyes of modern theologians, began to breathe new life into the dry bones of the church. Pietists rediscovered spontaneous prayer, Bible study, song and encouraged lay leadership outside the church. The Conventicle Act in Sweden had forbidden services outside the church or services led by anyone but ordained clergy. Per Andersson was a lay preacher in the Center City settlement.

Perhaps the oldest schoolhouse in the settlement, this structure stood at the southwest corner of the present Lutheran parsonage property in Center City.

Founders 18

much controversy, the siting of the church on the peninsula in 1857 brought together the many factions of Lutherans within the colony. Its location in the middle of the settlement provided a beginning for the town, and its central location in the settlement may have provided the town with its eventual name, Center City, the name given to it in 1857 when Svensson had it platted.

Moving On:

By 1855 the colony had a population of almost 500 and could be said to be firmly planted. A church had been founded, a school built, and a town born. It's curious to note, however, that after traveling thousands of miles and enduring the hardships connected with carving a new home out of the wilderness, only one of the original settlers chose to remain in the colony at Center City. Within a decade, the others had left: Viklund resettled almost immediately in Taylors Falls; Andersson moved around to a number of places before settling finally about thirty miles to the west at Cambridge; Rattig, now married, had gone to Colorado; and Berg had emigrated twenty-five miles northwest to the Fish Lake settlement. Of the founding party only Svensson remained. A half-brother of Per Andersson, Daniel Lindstrom, who arrived in 1853 and settled westward across the lake on a spot now named for him, also remained in the area. His farm was located where the Dinnerbel restaurant now stands.

Why did the original settlers move on? Was it the cholera epidemic of 1854? The economic panic of 1857? More probably it was the continuing religious controversy. And knowing that Per Andersson's ancestors themselves had emigrated from Finland to Sweden—as had those of Norelius and many other Norrlanders—and that 135 years later the descendents of the Andersson party can be found from Connecticut (Berg) to California (Andersson) may suggest that something even more powerful was at work, an inner force that drove them and perhaps drives many of us to seek what is on the other side of the next hill.

These, then, were the founders of the Center City colony: Per Andersson, the leader, and his family; Anders Svensson and family; Per Berg and family; Peter Viklund and family; and Andersson's hired man, Daniel Rattig. Others soon followed, but the original Andersson party was the group that inspired Moberg's stories which have so gripped the imaginations of generations of Swedes and others.

Daniel Lindstrom and his wife, Johanna Peterson. 1866.

1850 Territorial Census

Falls St. Croix Precinct, 14th August 1850

12	15	BISHOP, Thornton	30	M		Laborer	New York
		Abigail	22	F	H		Minnesota
		Henry	4	M	H		Minnesota
		Charles	3	M	H		Minnesota
13	16	HOLMES, William	31	M		Laborer	New York
		Mary	20	F			Minnesota
		SHORTWELL, Thomas	35	M		Lumberman	Scotland
		KAVENAUGH, Peter	30	M		Laborer	Michigan
14	17	BROWN, John	36	M		Laborer	New York
		Mary	28	F			New York
		SCOTT, Ira	22	M		Laborer	Maine
		COLLINS, P. G.	35	M		Laborer	Ireland
		CROCKETT, C.	30	M		Laborer	New York
15	18	COMER, Patrick	60	M		Indian trader	Ireland
		Susan	50	F	H		Wisconsin
		George	22	M	H		Minnesota
		Mary	18	F	H		Minnesota
16	19	COMER, Patrick (Jr.)	24	M	H	Indian trader	Wisconsin
		Frances	20	F	H		Wisconsin
17	20	COLBY, William	30	M		Lumberman	Maine
		Salina	18	F			Virginia
		Catherine	11	F			Virginia
		Charles	12	M			Virginia
		George	10	M			Illinois
		JEWETTE, John	29	M		Laborer	Maine
		RICHERSON (RICHARDSON), William	21	M		Laborer	Maine
		MOWER, Louis	22	M		Laborer	New York
		NICHOLS, Daniel	23	M		Laborer	Canada
		LAMARE, Joseph	21	M		Laborer	Canada
18	21	MORTON, L. S.	34	M		Laborer	New York
		ROSS, Jerimiah	35	M		Laborer	New York
		Sarah	18	F			Indiana
		Susan	9/12	F			Wisconsin
		LAMERS (LAMMERS), Frederick	22	M		Laborer	Germany
19	22	BARLOW, Louis	37	M		Blacksmith	Massachusetts
		Caroline	7	F			Vermont
		Roxanna	5	F			Wisconsin
		John L.	3	M			Missouri
		BAYSE, Matilda	22	F			Canada
		Silas	3	M			Canada
		TURNER, Charles	23	M		Laborer	Connecticut
		DAUBNY, John	25	M		Lumberman	Connecticut
		CARRIER, Walter	30	M		Lumberman	New York
		LEAVY, Ambrose	25	M		Laborer	Maine
		Stillman	23	M		Laborer	Maine
		HICKERSON, John	23	M		Laborer	Ohio
		CLARK, John W.	35	M		Laborer	New York
		WOODRUFF, Samuel	30	M		Laborer	Ohio
		ARLAR, Peter	25	M		Laborer	Canada
		GONON (GONNER), John	28	M		Blacksmith	Missouri
		BLAIR, William	35	M		Laborer	Scotland
		WEATER, George B.	24	M		Laborer	Indiana
		CRAWFORD, William	40	M		Laborer	Maine
		HITCHCOCK, E. R.	25	M		Laborer	Missouri
		MYERS, Henry	25	M		Laborer	Germany
		WINTERS, William	25	M		Laborer	Germany
		KISER, George	30	M		Laborer	Germany
		TAYLOR, Nathan C. D.	38	M		Lumberman	New Hampshire
		STOTMAN, Nicholas	30	M		Laborer	Germany
		BOWERS, Mr.	35	M		Laborer	Germany

Lars Peter Sjolin, a servant of Per Andersson, arrived in the settlement in the summer of 1851, some months after the original colonists.

In Their Own Words

A good check on the writing of history is that offered by the testimony of those who lived during or within living memory of the incident involved. Thus far, this history has considered contemporary newspaper accounts of the day, census and land records and, in addition to other histories touching upon the subject, the journals and other writings of Erik Norelius, a member of the Andersson party and a frequent visitor to the colony who was, in the summer of 1854, its first teacher. Norelius, 17 at the time of the crossing, changed Swedish money into American for his fellow travelers upon their arrival in New York. He is a candidate as a model for the fictional Karl Oskar's younger brother Robert, who performed the same, money-changing task. To Norelius' eyewitness account and memories we now consider additional testimony, including autobiographical writings, memoirs, sailing ship passenger lists, emigration papers, citizenship documents and other biographical materials which may help us better know and understand the people who founded Center City and the lives they led. Almost all accounts in this section are written by those within living memory of the founding of the colony. The words are theirs.

Joris Pell Per Anderson

Carin Andersson, Per's wife

Kristina Andersson was the first white child born in the settlement.

PER ANDERSSON

Per Andersson, the founder of the Center City colony, left the growing settlement in 1856. Before his departure he helped to found the Chisago Lake Evangelical Swedish Lutheran Church which still exists, had seen his wife Carin give birth to the first white child, Kristina, in the colony, had helped to build a school, and witnessed the building of a "new Scandia in the wilderness" that novelist Fredericka Bremer had prophesized during her 1850 trip to the Minnesota Territory.

From Center City, Andersson moved to Red Wing where his close friend, Erik Norelius, had started a church at Vasa. From Freeborn county he moved on, eventually settling in Cambridge, another Swedish settlement some thirty miles west of Chisago Lakes. There, on the banks of the Rum River, he lived with his son, Daniel, who was to serve six terms as a representative in the Minnesota State legislature before moving to California. The Andersson farm was located on the east side of the Rum, approximately where Highway 95 now crosses the river. Following an old-country custom, the Andersson's summer pasture was located upland from the farm, in this instance, across the river where the cows could be observed through the stands of willow and birch as they grazed. A rope bridge spanned the river. On an early autumn day in 1881 Per Andersson set out to check the cows on the west bank. He never returned. What happened is not clear, but his body was discovered days later floating downstream in the Rum. The year before, Per Viklund, another of the original party, who had moved to Anoka in 1860, also drowned in the Rum River. It's noteworthy that novelist Moberg, whose books made legends of the Andersson party, suffered the same fate, drowning in his native Sweden.

Per Andersson's account of the settlement at Chisago Lake which he founded. In it, Andersson writes of his party coming to Swede (Chisago) Lake in 1851. He locates the settlement nine English miles from Taylors Falls and thirty miles from Stillwater. He notes that four families were in the first group: his and that of Per Berg from Halsingland; one family from Angermanland, the Viklunds; and one from Ostergotland, the Anders Svenssons. There is no date on the writing which was found with the diary of Erik Norelius. Moberg's fictional emigrants, by contrast, came not from northern Sweden, as did most of the Andersson party, but from the south, Smoland, Moberg's own home territory.

A brief personal account of the nativity, parentage and career of the son of Per and Carin Andersson.

DANIEL ANDERSON
(written in 1903)

Having reached an age when additional years means a decline and decrease in mental as well as physical vigor, and having a numerous progeny, some of whom, or whose posterity, may sometime become interested to know who their ancestors were; I have concluded to make the following notes, mostly from personal knowledge, but in part from the information obtained from what I consider reliable sources.

I was born in the parish of Hassela, Gefleborgs Lau, Sweden, February 3rd 1842. My parents, Peter (or Per) Anderson and Karin (Danielsdotter) were both decendents from the Finns who settled in different sections of Northern Sweden, probably several centuries ago.

My parents were the owners of a backwoods farm of considerable extent, but of little utility for agricultural purposes, being composed largely of rock-bound wilds. (Containing a large amount of timber, however, which later became a source of wealth to those who came into possession.)

My father was a person of acknowledged quiet disposition and good character, more contemplative than energetic, credulous and accommodating; a good citizen and poor financier.

While he had no "schooling," he was an ardent reader and good writer and fairly well posted on general topics.

My mother (still alive in 1903) is by nature energetic and vehement and vindictive, and by far more prudent of the two.

During my early childhood my parents were neither rich nor poor—rather among the better lotted of their class and unless I am misinformed, the poor and unfortunate did not often call on them for assistance in vain.

When I was 8 years of age my parents made preparations to emmigrate to the United States. (Their real property was then sold for the sum of three thousand five hundred (3500) Ricks-daler, and only 25 years later it had increased about thirty-fold to more than one hundred thousand.) In those early days, before transportation companies and steamship lines were established, and before a foot of Railway had been built in Sweden, and comparatively little in the United States (not any west of Chicago) a journey from the interior

Daniel Andersson, son of Per and Carin, who served in the Minnesota legislature six times as a representative from Isanti County.

of Sweden to the central portion of the American continent (Minnesota) was not a matter of two or three weeks, as at present, but was in our case, a matter of seventy-seven (77) days (11 weeks) sailing in the same vessel, from the time we embarked, at Gefle, until we landed at New York, while the entire time consumed in actual travel and unavoidable delays, in making the journey to Rock Island, Ill., was seventeen (17) weeks, or one hundred and nineteen days.

A few months respite in the journey, and its continuation the next spring, towards the head waters of the Mississippi river consumed nearly the entire twelve months in reaching the final destination, viz: Chisago Lake, Minn., the forest covered shores of which had up to that time been unmolested by white men.

At the time of our arrival (in the spring of 1851), the family consisted of Father and Mother, my elder brother Andrew, myself, and two sisters, Helen and Ingrid Cajsa (later called Kate).

It is probably needless to say that my boyhood days, in a wild new country, a family without resources, except Father's labor, could not be other than a period of poverty. Not to the extent of actual suffering for want of food and shelter but conveniences, or in cultivation of civilities or social refinements, and last but not least, the lack of school facilities, by reason of which I have endured the inconveniences of a lifetime.

In the fall of 1856, and when the new settlement began to develop the principal features of civilization, my parents moved again, and after spending the winter in the then village of Redwing (where I attended confirmation class before now, Dr. E. Norelius), they moved to Freeborn County, in the south part of this state, where only a few families had preceeded us the previous year. While conditions met with there differed widely from our experiences in the heavy timber in Chisago County, the change in the first instance was not for the better. Shelter for both men and beasts are not easily procured in a prairie district seventy-five miles from nearest lumber supply, by men without means.

But not only that, our bread supply, or its substitute cornmeal, had to come from the Mississippi River 75 miles away, or from near Decorah in Iowa nearly 100 miles away, where some of the settlers had corn to sell, and in the spring of 1858, which was a very late one, when the winter supply had been consumed, the impassable condition of the "Sloughs" low and mirey places in the prairie, where the "sod" had become decayed by the travel of the previous year, rendered the passage with teams nearly impossible and the conse-

Andrew Andersson, older brother of Daniel, who died of pneumonia at Ft. Snelling in 1862 while serving in the army.

quence was a condition nearly akin to famine. As long as there was a panful of meal in anybody's house, it was divided to aid those who had none. One year's crop, however, changed the condition respecting provisions and food to one of plenty.

Prior to the age 15, I had been too puny and small to be of any account to work but now as I gained in size, I became of more utility in the general struggle for existence and the two months term of public school, held in the summer for the benefit of the smaller scholars, done me no good when I had not time to attend. When I was eighteen years old I worked away from home enough to earn a few clothes, and during the winter months, for two seasons, I attended a private school where we each paid tuition. Probably but few persons convicted of felony feel more keenly the sentence imposed than I did the self imposed task of expressing my ignorance in a schoolroomful of mostly grown up young people. The ice once broken, it was my intention to devote my winters to school and thus secure an education, for which I felt some craving; but alas, that was not to be. The first two years of the Southern Rebellion had brought matters to that critical point, when all men whose loyalty and patriotism outweighed their personal interests, felt it their duty to rally around the Flag. On returning at the close of the war, after three years of service, physically badly damaged for manual labor by reason of severe overheating, or sunstroke, I found my parents and younger sisters (my elder brother died in the Army) much in need of my assistance which together with my own mistaken notion—that I was too old to commence going to school again—caused me to make the decision which I have ever since regarded as the mistake of my life, viz: give up the hope of securing school instruction. Many and bitter have been the regrets, during a lifetime, over the lack of preparation for the opportunities that have presented themselves!

Being by nature neither mercenary nor energetic and being through my childhood and youth accustomed and trained by circumstances, to self denials and sacrifices, and finally when at the threshold of my majority—take a three years' course of initiation in risking even existence itself for thirteen dollars per month, for public good, it seems to be but a natural consequence that in later years the tree would lean the way the twig was bent. (More interested in, and more adapted to politics and some insight into public matters, than for acquiring property or saving money.) Shortly before my 28th birthday I entered a life partnership with Caroline Peterson, also of Finnish extraction, from Loosparish, Sweden, a girl ten years my junior and of likely appearance, very energetic and industrious, and as I have been fully convinced, very determined. Much more prudent and provident in business matters than myself, and also much more exacting and uncompromising, in small matters as well as large.

Without going into detail, I feel justified in saying that probably very few couples have lived together with such universal incompatibility of temper and judgements, making it correspondingly difficult to avoid shipwreck. Poverty, a large family and a lucky go easy husband, are probably sufficient causes to keep a nervous and overworked woman in as uncomfortable state of mind as the husband has to endure, whose lot it is to be constantly criticised, lectured, and admonished, not only for his own acts and omissions, but for those of his parents before him, as well. In regard to vocation and means of livlihood, I think my experiences are as varied as could be wished for. Breaking the prairie and subduing the forest for cultivation are tasks with which my earliest memories are associated, cutting grass with the scythe, reaping grain with the "cradle"—and raking and binding it by hand, has made my body ache with fatigue in years gone by.

I have felled the pines in the forest, and I have assisted in floating them to market. I have dispensed general merchandise over the counter for others, and for myself. I have served on School boards, Town boards, and as U.S. Postmaster. I have served as Justice of the Peace, Notary Public, Enumerator in taking U. S. Census, have served on the County Board, and as County Surveyor, as Deputy Clerk of Court, and several terms as County Auditor, and the same as Judge of Probate; and a half a dozen times as Representative in State Legislature; besides several times as State Land Appraiser, and Member of the State Board of Equalization. This would seem sufficient to warrant the conclusion that I have had an insatiable greed for public positions; but such is not the case; at least not to the extent of being a constant hanger-on, or a weather-cock, to suit all winds, but I have been in this as in other matters, a creature of Circumstance. In the early years of this County, very few men had any time, inclination, or qualifications for office. Under those conditions I was initiated as an experiment, and not having purposely violated the confidence placed in me I have ever since been regarded as available for almost any emergency - notwithstanding the present abundance of better qualified material.

Of course it would be absurd to suppose that a great variety of functions could be, or have been filled or performed to a high degree of efficiency, by an untutored ruralist like myself, but it is also surprising that in the absence of any preparation, or acquired ability, my efforts have not been *less* successful than they really have.

ANDERS SVENSSON

Anders Svensson is properly called the proprietor of Center City, since he had the town platted in 1857. One rather amazing story that has come out of the early history of the settlement concerns his wife, Cajsa Lisa, who set out one day in 1852 in search of cows who had wandered away:

From R. Gronberger, Svenskkarna St. Croixdalen

The wife of Anders Swensson made this year a very unpleasant trip. One fine morning she went out in the woods to look for her cows. In the tall grass and brush she could trace the direction which they had passed. She followed their path through the wilderness without knowing in what direction she was going. A woman in our days with less determination and a less stout heart would probably have given up such a task as looking for cows in the wild woods where wild animals and prowling Indians were the only living things to be encountered. Not so Mrs. Swensson. She would under no circumstances lose her good milchers, so she continued all day without finding them. Toward evening, in the vicinity of where Vasa, in the Marine settlement, was later located, she met a man who said that he had met a pair of cows, but that was so long before, that there was no possibility for her to overtake them. The man being afraid lest she was going to get lost if she continued her search in the dark, offered to build a fire at which they could "camp" during the night. Thanking him for the offer she, however, declined it, and, having received a few matches to be used in case she would need to build a fire and camp out alone, she went. Before it was entirely dark, she was lucky enough to reach the house of a farmer in the neighborhood of Marine. The farmer had caught and locked in the so-eagerly-sought-for-cows. The distance from this farmer's to her home was fifteen miles, as the bird flies, and as the cows' path probably did not lay in such a direct course, Mrs. Swensson had walked a much longer distance. The following day she returned over the same route but this time driving the cows before her. We must admire Mrs. Swensson's energy and endurance all the more when we are informed that she bore a fine girl two months later. This child was born November 22, 1852; baptized by A.M. Dahlhjelm, receiving the name of Christine Mathilda.

ANDREW PORTER
(written about 1932)

Although he was not a member of the original Andersson party, the following memoir of Andrew "Andy" Porter is included here because it offers one of the best eyewitness accounts of the settlement available. It was written about 1932.

Having been asked to put into writing as much as I can remember of the early life and experiences of myself and our family relations from pioneer times until present, I leave the following reminiscences which are not claimed to contain all what might be of interest for later generations to know about their ancestors, but it contains all what the writer can remember from his own knowledge and what he has heard from older people.

My parents came to this country from Sweden in 1853 and 1854.

My mother came in 1853 from Furuby parish in Kronoberg's province in company with her half brother Anders P. Glader and his family, consisting of his wife Elin, and five children, Carl, Gustaf, Helena, Sofia and Maria. The trip was very tedious and troublesome, it was said that it took several months just to cross the Atlantic Ocean, and after landing here they were taken over the inland lakes and by horseteam from Chicago to some place on the Mississippi River and then by steamboat to Stillwater. Here my mother stayed for a while and worked as domestic in the family of Dr. Carli. She afterwards went to Marine Mills, or as it is now called, Marine-on-the-St. Croix, and worked in a hotel called Marine House owned by one Mr. Lightner. From there she moved to Chisago Lake to locate permanently as a farmer's wife. Uncle Glader went directly with his family to Chisago Lake and settled close to the lake on the south shore where he worked up a farm and made his permanent home. His wife must have died either on the voyage from the old country or soon after their arrival here, because not long after they came here he married Anna Nordstrom with whom he had six children: John, Solomon, Oscar, Eugene, Louis, Victoria and Christine. After some years Carl Glader bought some land, worked up a farm and built a house about half a mile south of Uncle Glader's place. The farm where William Nichlason now lives.

My father, (whose name in the old country was Anders Jaenson) came here in 1854 from Tavelaas parish in the province of Kronobergs Lan Sweden. He started out accompanied by his father, (Jaen

Anders Jaensson Porter, an early settler in the colony, whose descendents still reside in the area.

Aaronson), his wife and five children —Ingrid, Johan Gustaf, Solomon, Rebecca Christina, and Johana. After the usual troubles and tribulations connected with the crossing of the Atlantic in an old sail boat, they were safely landed at Quebec, Canada. Here it was reported that cholera was prevalent in this country and the captain of the ship advised the passengers to stay in Quebec over winter and not go any further until the following spring, but my father, anxious to arrive at destination as soon as possible, started out and when they came to Chicago his wife died and she was buried in the cemetery of the Lutheran Immanuel Church. She was a sister of Jonas Haraldson, that lived about three miles north of Center City some years ago.

From Chicago the journey was continued by horseteam to Galena, Illinois, and from there by steamboat to Stillwater. While on the boat my grandfather died and his remains were enclosed in a box nailed together and without ceremony dug down in the river bank. No one has ever known since just where this took place.

Upon arriving at Stillwater my father at once started out with his five children by horse team through the wild woods for Chisago Lake which was from the beginning the goal set for the journey.

Here my father purchased a fraction of 57 acres on the east shore of the lake in Section 2, Township 33 North, Range 20 West. This fraction had previously belonged to one Porter who had recently died and he had built a small shanty out of round logs and cleared 2 acres between the shanty and the lake shore. some more land adjoining this fraction was afterwards bought from the government.

Among the early settlers here a good many had or took the name "Johnson" as that was considered to be a pretty good American expression of their former name, and my father was one of them, but the folks began to call him Porter, or Anders to Porter's to distinguish him from the many Johnsons in the community. This became more and more general and father finally adopted that name, and it has since been the family name.

My father being a widower having five children that needed care, it was necessary for him to have a housekeeper, and an elderly couple, afterwards known as Petter and Elin pa udden, that had come in his company from the old country, stayed with him until he, in 1855, married Helena Nilson, previously mentioned as half sister of A.P. Glader.

In this union seven children in all were born —the first two were twins, a boy and a girl, the girl was either still born or she died immediately after birth —the boy lived long enough to be baptized, when he was named Carl Adolph —but he died soon after. Where they were buried is not known to the writer. The other children were; Frans Adolph, Emma Christina, Johannis, Amanda and Esther — reference to whom will be made further on.

The log shanty being too small for a large family, my father erected a two story building of hewed logs on the same spot where the house now is, but after having been occupied over one winter it burned in the spring of 1860. The writer then being about a year and a half old was carried by his mother through a room all in flames and dropped on the ground, where he was picked up by his sister Johanna and taken away from the heat. My mother then went to the back side of the house and knocked in a window and succeeded in getting out a couple of large Swedish chests containing some bed clothes and other dry goods —all the rest in the house was consumed by the flames.

The log shanty which then stood close to where the barn now is was moved to a place about two rods north of where the burned house had been. It was then used until the present house on the farm was built the year 1869.

When the Civil War (which is sometimes called the war of the rebellion) broke out in 1861, the two Glader brothers and John Porter enlisted in the U.S. Army to fight for the preservation of the Union. Solomon Porter being the youngest enlisted some time later. They all served to the end of the war when they were honorably discharged and came home. They were then for some years working in the lumber woods in winter time and on the river driving and rafting logs in summer time, until harvest time, when they usually went to work for prairie farmers during the harvest and threshing. Carl Glader was a part of the time busy in opening up a farm on his land and after having built a house he married my oldest half sister, Mary. While they lived on this farm their oldest son, Ulysses Lincoln, was born.

Gustaf Glader, in partnership with P.O. Hall, rented a farm at Mann Valley near River Falls, Wisconsin. While there he married Rebecca Porter. Their first son, Bernadotte Sheridan died when he was a baby and was buried in the Glader Cemetery. About this time P.O. Hall married Mary Glader, and to them two daughters, Minnie and Hattie, were born. When through farming at River Falls they all came back to Chisago Lake and P.O. Hall bought the farm of Carl Glader and about 1870 the Glader brothers and the two Porter brothers moved to Kandiyohi County and located —John and Solomon Porter two miles south of Stockholm (now Atwater), Carl Glader five miles and Gustaf seven miles south, near Lake Elizabeth.

After having opened up a farm and built a house, John Porter married Mary Erickson of Spring Lake; they had several children, some of whom died while young. Elmer the oldest died before he had grown up, John's wife died while they lived on the farm. He later sold the farm and moved to Atwater where he died. The only children of the family now living are Gustaf and Mabel now living at Dassel. Gustaf is married and has no children —Mabel has never been married and has and is now making her home with Gustaf and his wife.

Solomon Porter located on a part of the land bought in partnership with John and married Lutina Lindquist, a local teacher. They had six children —Oliver, Milton, Florence, Lester, Harold, Walter Gertrude and Myrtle. Oliver was for many years a practicing physician at Atwater, where he is now located is not known to the writer. Florence is married and lives somewhere in the east. The other three boys are not much known to the writer, only that they were doctors of medicine or dentists. Gertrude is married and when last heard of she lived at Montevideo. Myrtle is not married and is teaching on the west coast. Solomon served a number of years as County Treasurer of Kandiyohi County, he then lived in Willmar where he afterwards died.

After coming to Kandiyohi County five children, Franklin, Edwin, Lydia, Rebecca and Lutina were born in the Carl Glader family. Frank died in Minneapolis in October 1932, leaving a widow and no children. Ulysses and Edwin live near the coast —Lydia is married and lives in Minneapolis and among her children are a pair of twins, a boy and a girl. Rebecca died very young. Lutina is single and lives in Atwater, as far as is known. Sister Mary died while they lived on the farm.

In Gustaf Glader's family Sumner and Addie were born and when Sumner was grown up he became the owner of the farm and married. He soon thereafter sold the farm and moved to Atwater where he and his family now live. Sister Rebecca died while they lived on the farm; Addie lives with a family in Minneapolis and has never been married.

When they had disposed of their farms Carl and Gustaf Glader went out to the coast for a few years; they then came back to Atwater and stayed there until they died. Gustaf Glader served one term as Senator in the state legislature.

My youngest half sister Johanna worked as a domestic in several families in Minneapolis and married Peter Nelson, a cousin of the writer. They had one daughter, Edna, who after having married went to the state of Washington where her husband died many years ago. Nelson worked for many years as car cleaner and car inspector in the railroad yards in Minneapolis. Both Nelson and Johanna died long ago.

Helena Glader married one by the name of Church who died in the army during the war. They had three girls, Wealthy, Clementina, and Melvina, of who all are married and now living as far as is known to this writer. Helena afterwards married Nels Rosenquist. They lived on a farm in Kandiyohi County where they both died. They had several children, of whom only one, Minnie, is known to the writer. She is the wife of Alfred Bloom at Chisago City.

Sofia married C.P. Quist. They lived for some years on a farm at Chisago Lake, southeast of Chisago City. They later moved to Kandiyohi County and after a few years they moved to Thief River Falls and finally they came back to Atwater where they both died.

P.O. Hall, who had bought the farm of Carl Glader, sold the farm and with his family located on a farm close to the city limits at Atwater. After a few years he sold this farm and moved into Atwater where Hall served as Postmaster a number of years. Here Mr. and Mrs. Hall and their daughter Minnie died, but Hattie, as far as is known, is married and still living.

Uncle A.P. Glader, was a man of unusual strength and endurance, and endured many hardships in life that he stood up under as if nothing unusual had happened. When a young boy he was herding stock for his parents. He discovered a small bunch of hay on the ground one day which he picked up to give to one of the animals, that he was herding. Under this bunch of hay a poisonous snake was concealed and bit the boy in the ball of his hand. The boy knowing that this meant sure death to him if the poison was allowed to spread in his system, he cut out a piece of the ball in his hand and laid it on a stump and watched it swell up. In this way his life was saved.

After he came to this country he was in many accidents, having arms and legs broken. He was badly crippled, one leg being considerably shorter than the other. One time when he was hauling hay the load tipped over on him and crushed him to the ground. He worked himself out of the hay, straightened out the sled and hayrack, reloaded the hay, took it home and unloaded the hay into the barn and said nothing about it. The writer once saw him light his pipe with a live coal that he took out of the stove with his fingers, and when the writer expressed his wonder that the fingers were not burned he took the coal in his hand and held it a while and his hand did not tremble.

When the first Swedish Lutheran Church was built at Center City, most of the work was performed by the church members—each one donating so many days of work without pay. Most of them being unaccustomed to this kind of work it was necessary to have someone to superintend the work to see to it that it was done right. For this job Uncle Glader was selected, and when the church was completed he was credited with having done a good job. After a long, active and useful life, he finally died at an old age.

John, the oldest son of the younger set, was married and had no children, and he was engaged in different kinds of work at several places. He never settled down to real home life. He died at about middle age. Upon the death of Uncle Glader, Solomon and his mother took hold of the farm work in real earnest and cared for the smaller children until they were grown up. Solomon finally became owner of the farm and married Anna Loise Andrews of Lindstrom. They had no children. Solomon soon thereafter moved to Lindstrom and in partnership with his brother-in-law, Charles Andrews and William Carlson of Center City, went into the lumber business under the firm name of Andrews, Carlson and Glader. Here the old lady died and after both of his partners had died Solomon sold out his business and together with his wife lived a retired life. He has served as trustee of the Lutheran Church at Center City and as President of the Security State Bank of Lindstrom. He died December 11, 1932.

Oscar is a widower and has no children. He lives in Minneapolis.

Victoria married August Schlemmer and they have no children. They conducted a summer resort for some years on an island near Chisago City. Victoria died a few years ago. Eugene is living on the coast as far as is known to the writer. Christine is doing laboratory work in Minneapolis. Louis died many years ago. He was never married.

When in its natural state this country for several miles around the lake was overgrown with heavy timber such as basswood, hard maple, elm, oak, ironwood and hickory and a dense undergrowth of different kinds of brush. This made very hard tedious work to clear the land for raising crops, but after this was done there were the roots in the ground and the stumps which it usually took from five to ten years to eradicate. The soil, however, was very productive and, especially on new fields, yielded good crops such as corn, potatoes, rutabagas, beans and some garden vegetables, which, — together with bread, homemade butter and cheese, milk, and home-butchered meat, constituted the means of subsistence. When coffee was used it was usually roasted at home and crushed with a large round bottle instead of running it through a grinder. With this roasted rye was mixed, and if sweetening was wanted maple syrup was used.

Fish were at that time abundant in the lake and fishing was usually left to the kids. The fishing tackle most used for catching sunfish was a homespun linen thread twisted double, one end tied to a pole and a common pin bent in the shape of a hook tied to the other end of the line. Some pickerel and bass were also caught by trolling and by setting nets.

Other winter clothes, especially the men's clothes, were made with homewoven cloth. This cloth was made with cotton yarn for warp and homespun woolen yarn for filling. The wool was carded and spun by hand at home. Father sometimes did some carding evenings, otherwise this work usually devolved on my mother. The writer does well remember how she, after having tucked us little ones away for our night's sleep, often kept the spinning wheel humming until near midnight. For outside clothes white warp and black filling was ordinarily used, and for underwear white was used exclusively. When weaving was completed a tailor was hired to come to the house and make the men's suits and the underclothes were made by my mother. All sewing was made by hand. The weaving loom in which this cloth was made is now in the possession of the writer.

My mother at all times used all her best efforts to have us well clad and protected from the cold and otherwise comfortable, and the writer will always keep her in thankful memory.

There being no natural hay meadows on our farm, father like many other farmers cut a good deal of hay on the meadows of the Sunrise River, 5 or 6 miles west from our farm. The hay was hauled home in winter time with ox team and many times it met with difficulties on account of the deep snow drifting and in some places piling up several feet high, so that a shovel sometimes had to be carried along to open the road. The writer was sometimes taken along on these trips to tramp down the hay as it was pitched onto the load. After starting for home was the usual time for taking lunch. This consisted of bread, homemade butter and cheese. This was sometimes frozen hard and some warm coffee to soften it up would have been appreciated, but the writer having good teeth and a hungry stomach managed to get outside of it without any trouble.

My father soon got tired of getting hay in this way so he reduced his stock to a number that could be taken care of with the hay raised at home. About this time my father had some hard maple cut up into cordwood on land that he intended to clear for cultivation. For the cutting of this wood one dollar per cord was paid. This wood was the following winter hauled with ox team to Taylors Falls and sold for two dollars per cord, cash, and sometimes $2.50 per cord, store goods. At this time the first oil lamp that was used in our house was bought. Kerosene oil at that time was $1.00 per gallon, but it was of a good deal better quality than the oil we are now getting, and had to be handled with care on account of its high explosive qualities. Up to this time homemade tallow candles had been used to light up the living room. When there was no more tallow to make candles with we had to get along with the light given out by an open fireplace in one corner of the room.

During the first years of settlement here Chippewa Indians were seen roaming around in the woods looking for game and early morning reports of their firearms was heard around the lake when they were hunting ducks. One day when my mother was baking bread some of these Indians came in and had a bunch of newly shot ducks and partridges and when they saw the newly baked bread that had been laid on the table to cool, they indicated by their signs that they wanted to trade their bunch of game for some bread. Mother gave them some bread and they left the bunch of game and went away, apparently well satisfied. These Indians were very friendly and they never did any harm to people or stock.

During the Sioux Indian uprising in the summer of 1862 the people of this community were much excited and scared by the many stories told and circulated here about the ravages of the enraged Indians. News at this time was very meager here, about the only paper that was read here at that time was a Swedish weekly called *"Hemlandet"* published at Chicago, Illinois. This paper had very little news about Minnesota and what news it did have from this state was usually too old to be worth anything, consequently the news about what was going on outside of this settlement was only talk and sometimes quesswork that afterwards proved untrue and erroneous. There was a story told that every house in the village of Sunrise had been burned and the people all killed by the Indians. Two men were sent to Sunrise on horseback to find out if this was true and when they came back they reported that from an adjoining hilltop they had seen the ruins of the burned buildings but not a living person. This added to the excitement and fear of folks here, but it was later found out that the men from here had not been near Sunrise but they had simply made up a story.

One afternoon it was discovered from our house that our neighbor Molin's barn was burning and the first thought was that the Indians had arrived and would soon be at our house, and our folks made haste to get ready to escape across the lake; but just as we reached the lake shore our dog "Carlo" gave up a howl that told us that somebody was approaching our house from the other side. This increased our fears as we thought sure it was the Indians coming, but presently there appeared on top of the hill a person whom my mother recognized as Molin's daughter. My mother asked her where the fire had come from. She answered by pointing upward toward the sky indicating the barn had been fired by lightning —a thunder shower was passing over.

One evening after dark a light was seen east from our house and it was taken to be an Indian camp fire where the Indians stayed overnight and would be ready to attack the adjoining farmhouses the following morning. Preparations were again made to escape across the lake but before we got ready to go the moon went up.

Many years ago the writer heard the following told by a farmer who lived 3 or 4 miles north of Center City. There had been an agreement made by the farmers that no one was to start an outside fire on a clearing or otherwise for fear that it might attract the attention of the Indians and if any such fire was seen after dark the folks that saw it should know that the Indians had arrived and had set fire to some farmhouses. A farmer in his neighborhood either disregarded this agreement or did not know anything about it. One evening he set fire to a brush pile on his clearing and another farmer who saw this fire from his house thought the Indians had arrived and made haste to hitch his horses to a homemade wooden truck, (it being the only vehicle on wheels he had), and with his family loaded on he started for Taylors Falls as fast as the horses could go. The wheels and axles being nothing but wood the axles soon got dry and commenced to give out the squeaks so characteristic to that kind of vehicle, and pretty soon several axles gave out their noise in their different keys at the same time. It being a still and quiet evening this noise, together with the rumbling of the truck, was heard distances away and aroused the people along the road. L.K. Stannard, who lived about a mile this side of Taylors Falls happened to be out at the time and as he heard the peculiar noise while it was some distance away he could not make out what it was. After a while the truck with its passengers whizzed by at high speed and then he understood that it was some farmer trying to escape from the approaching Indians, but the Indians never came.

By this time excitement was running high and it was agreed that something had to be done for protection, as stories were continuously in circulation about the wild ravages of the Indians. A large number, if not all the settlers, took their refuge to an island in the lake called lonne (maple island). This island is located about half a mile across the lake from our home and when the lake was high it was entirely surrounded by water, but when the lake was low it was connected with the main and a sandbar at the south end of the island. At the intersection of this sand bar a breastwork or safety wall was built out of round logs on the outside and dirt thrown up against the wall on the island to hold the logs in place. A mark in the ground can be seen now where his breastwork was built seventy years ago. Having thus fortified themselves the best they could, they went to work and built a number of temporary shacks or shanties of different styles and modes. The writer does well remember that some of these shacks had roofs thatched with rye straw in old Swedish fashion. To this place the settlers took their families and some provisions. Those that had guns of any kind took them along. Others brought pitchforks, axes, butcher knives and anything that could be used as a weapon for defense against the expected Indians.

A breastwork was also built at Center City between the church and the cemetery. On top of this breastwork a howitzer was placed that it was thought would scare the Indians out of sight with the tremendous roar it made when discharged. This breastwork was afterwards taken down and the howitzer taken up to the church where the writer saw it lying on the ground for years afterwards. It was later bursted when given an overcharge of gunpowder at a Fourth of July celebration, but no one was hurt.

To quell this Indian uprising that had caused so much excitement and fear among the settlers, the Third and Seventh Regiments of Minnesota Volunteers, who at this time were home on furlough from the Civil War, were called out and under the command of Col. Sibley captured about 2,000 prisoners of whom about 400 were sentenced by court martial to be hanged. Of these 38 were executed at Mankato, December 26, 1862, - the remainder having been pardoned by President Lincoln. (See "Fifty Years in the Northwest" by W.H.C. Folsom, page 5)

Among the soldiers known to the writer who took part in this expedition and who were detailed to—armed with muskets and bayonets—stand guard over the prisoners during the trial and execution were father Longquist, Carl and Gustaf Glader, John O. Porter, and C.P. Quist. No doubt there were others among these soldiers from this community but it is not known to the writer who they were. Thus ended this excitement that had caused so much disturbance among the people and the settlers devoted their time and energy toward improving their homes and opening and improving roads, especially between the lake and the St. Croix River.

About this time a stave factory was built at Chisago City where staves were made out of oak bolts that were hauled in by the farmers. These staves were to begin with hauled by horse team to Franconia and then shipped to some place south where they were made up into barrels. Later a steamboat was built by which the staves were shipped to the southeast end of the lake and from there were hauled to Franconia. Ordinarily the staves were landed just south of our farm, but when the lake was highest the steamboat went around the Holmberg place by way of "Loras Ranna" (Lorens Creek) into Ogren lake where the staves were landed a few rods from the wagon road. At that time the water was so high in the lake that the steamboat passed with its load unobstructed over a sand bar that connects a little island known as "Korko" (Church Island) with the mainland. This island is located in front of where we lived at that time and the writer many times watched the steamboat pass over the sand bar.

The emigration permit of Anders Jaensson Porter.

41 In Their Own Words

Emigration Permit No. 1 From Tafelsas

A farmer, Anders Jaensson from Tafelsas, - and his wife Katrina Haraldsdotter, born, he, September 15, 1822, she December 11, 1819, both from Tafelsas congregation. Now they move to North America with testimony of moderate Christian knowledge, a reverent use of the Means of Grace and wholesome joy Partook of the Lord's Supper last on 5th inst. They have regularly attended the annual examinations and are enrolled for the current year.

Their children who also accompany them are:

Daughter,	Ingrid Maria	born August 26, 1841	
Son,	Johan Gustaf	born May 1, 1843	
Son,	Solomon	born December 31, 1844	(All in
Daughter,	Rebecca Christina	born December 26, 1846	Tafelsas)
Daughter,	Johanna	born June 4, 1850	

The three oldest children read moderately well according to their age; the children as well as parents are polite.

May the protection and grace of the Most High follow them on the adventurous journey which lies ahead.

Tafelsas parsonage in Kinnesvald Harad (district) in Kronobergs lan (province). March 21, 1854

>   Sec.
>   N. Wislander
>   P.L. (Pastor loci)

Came to America November 1854

Present wife Helena Nilsdotter born December 18, 1823, Furuby, Kronobergs lan (province). Came to America September 1853,

Translated by Ruth Porter Sandstedt with help of H.E. Sandstedt and Swedish-English Dictionary.

>   July 19, 1962

Note:
   The above, Anders Jaensson, settled about two miles south of Center City and later changed his name to Anders Porter.

Another early settler was MATTIS BENGTSON who arrived in the colony in 1853. His descendents, as those of Porter, still live in the Chisago Lakes area.

MEMOIRS OF MATTIS BENGTSON
(written on August 3, 1895)

My paternal grandfather was a soldier, a cavalry man (that was so that landowners on estates could keep both horse and man in wartimes as well as peace times). His name was Nels Modes, he died at 50 years of age.

My father had two brothers, Tuve Hall and Mons Hall, and one sister Nila. Tuve Hall had been a soldier a few years and died 50 years of age. My father Bengt was the eldest and lived long after the others, if my memory serves me right. He reached the high age of 85. He was born in 1788 in Krusboda, Orkna-socken.

Father often spoke at burials and had a fine singing voice. He was always very glad to sing.

My mother was born in Hogsma, Glimokra in 1785 and died at 65 years of age.

I am the youngest of six children. I had two brothers and three sisters. Nils was born in 1810, Per was born in 1821 and died at age 49. Sister Elsa was born in 1813 and died at age 73. Kierste was born in 1816 and died at age 23. Bengta was born in 1818 and was married to Lars Munson. They and all their children perished in the ocean when the ship on which they were passengers (on their way to America) struck a rocky cliff and sank near the coast of New Foundland in 1857.

I was born on January 18 in 1826 in Krusboda Torp. My father was a carpenter by trade and I helped him with anything I could do, which was not very much, as I was mostly a farmer and tilled the soil. I worked very hard until I was 21 years of age, when I went into army training at Gungby Hede. After that I began to do carpentry and cabinet work in the winters and building construction in the summers until August 1852 when I journeyed to America. I was then 26 years of age.

From the day I left my home in Sweden until the day I reached Knoxville, Illinois was exactly 6 weeks. We were 21 days on the ocean in a sailboat. I stayed in Knoxville until February 1853 when I went to Moline, Illinois where I stayed a couple of months, then journeyed by boat to Saint Paul. There I met an American called Swede who had a contract for state road work on the east side of the

Mattis Bengtson, an early settler.

In Their Own Words

Mississippi river. He spoke Swedish fluently.

In the fall of 1853 I came to this Swedish settlement, which was only 3 years old (Center City). During this winter I worked in a saw mill, and when spring came in 1854 I began to chop down the trees on the land I picked by Little Lake.

When fall came I went to work in the woods and was there until April 1855.

After a few days Karna (Nils dotter) came who later became my wife on May 27, 1855. We became acquainted in Sweden and she traveled until she found me. I believe she was sent to find me.

My maternal grandfather was born in Tramboda and grandmother also was born in Tramboda. Grandfather Nils Bjornson was a landowner a few years in Edemor, which they sold and moved to Flygbade where he had good work and he prospered fairly well. He left his home to his sons Hakan and Nicklas and died at 80 years of age. His wife (my grandmother) died at a little over 60 years of age. They left 7 children, namely Per, Hakan, Nicklas, Mattis, Bengta, Maria and mother.

At the time we started to farm here, we had a democratic government until 1861, when the Civil War broke out and times became very hard. A yard of calico cloth then sold for 50 cents and everything else went up accordingly. During that time it was not pleasant to be called father to a large number of children, but I was thankful to God who let me stay home from the war, but it cost me plenty.

As soon as the war was over times got better till everything went up so high that people were dissatisfied with conditions and wanted the best of everything, and now it will take more than 10 years to restore the land again. I was drafted into the army shortly before the end of the war and returned home from Fort Snelling in 1865.

Erik Norelius, the first teacher in the colony during the summer of 1854. His diaries provide much of the surviving eye-witness accounts of the journey of the Andersson party.

SIX GENERATIONS OF NORELIUS' IN CHISAGO COUNTY 1850-1986

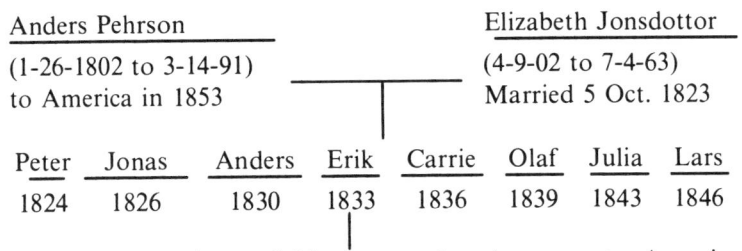

Anders Pehrson	Elizabeth Jonsdottor
(1-26-1802 to 3-14-91)	(4-9-02 to 7-4-63)
to America in 1853	Married 5 Oct. 1823

Peter	Jonas	Anders	Erik	Carrie	Olaf	Julia	Lars
1824	1826	1830	1833	1836	1839	1843	1846

Erik Andersson changed his name when he came to America in 1850, apparently after a popular pastor with that name who served Hassela Parish in 1850. Erik (Andersson) Norelius was born in Hassela, Sweden on 26 October 1833 and died in Vasa, Minnesota on 15 March 1916. As a student pastor he held the first regular services at the Center City colony in 1854. He later founded Gustavus Adolphus College in 1862, an orphanage and many churches and helped organize the Augustana Synod of which he was president for 18 years. Editor of the first Swedish newspaper in Minnesota, the *Posten,* he also edited *Hemlandet,* the first Swedish newspaper in America. In 1903 and 1910 he was knighted by the King of Sweden.

Theodore	Leonard	Marion Sigfried
an attorney in Washington, D.C., he drowned in North Center Lake in 1889	a bartender on San Francisco Barbary Coast	slated to be Republican gubernatorial candidate at time of his death from cancer in 1926

Erik	Theodore	Paul	Charlotte
b 1908 Pressman at paper in Lindstrom	b 1909 Editor, Chisago County Press, 1932-65. Knighted by King of Sweden in 1961	b 1910 Lindstrom Postmaster	Lindstrom

Neil

Blaine	Bart	Brice
b 1957	b 1959	b 1960

Jay

Brian	Bradley
b 1972	b 1975

CITIZENSHIP

ERIK NORELIUS' father Anders Per (Peter) Norelius arrived in the Center City Colony in 1854 and took out his citizenship papers that year.

I Anders Peter Norelius do upon my oath declare that I am fifty-two years old, that I first arrived in the United States on or about the 14th day of November A.D. 1853, and that I have continued to reside in the United States ever since that time; and that it is my bona fide intention to become a citizen of the United States, and do hereby renounce all allegiances and fidelity—to every foreign prince, potentate, state or sovereignty—and particularly all allegiance and fidelity to Oscar, first King of Sweden to whom I lately owed allegiance.

      Anders Per Norelius

Subscribed & Sworn before me this tenth day of October A.D. 1854
L.K. Stannard Deputy Clerk

Territory of Minnesota
County of Chisago   ss

I Anders Peter Norelius do solemnly swear that I will support the Constitution of the United States and the act of Congress organizing the territorial Government of Minnesota so help me, God.

      Anders Per Norelius

Subscribed & Sworn before me this tenth day of October A.D. 1854
L.K., Stannard
Deputy Clerk of Dist. Court
Chisago County Minn. Territory

In Their Own Words

47 Center City

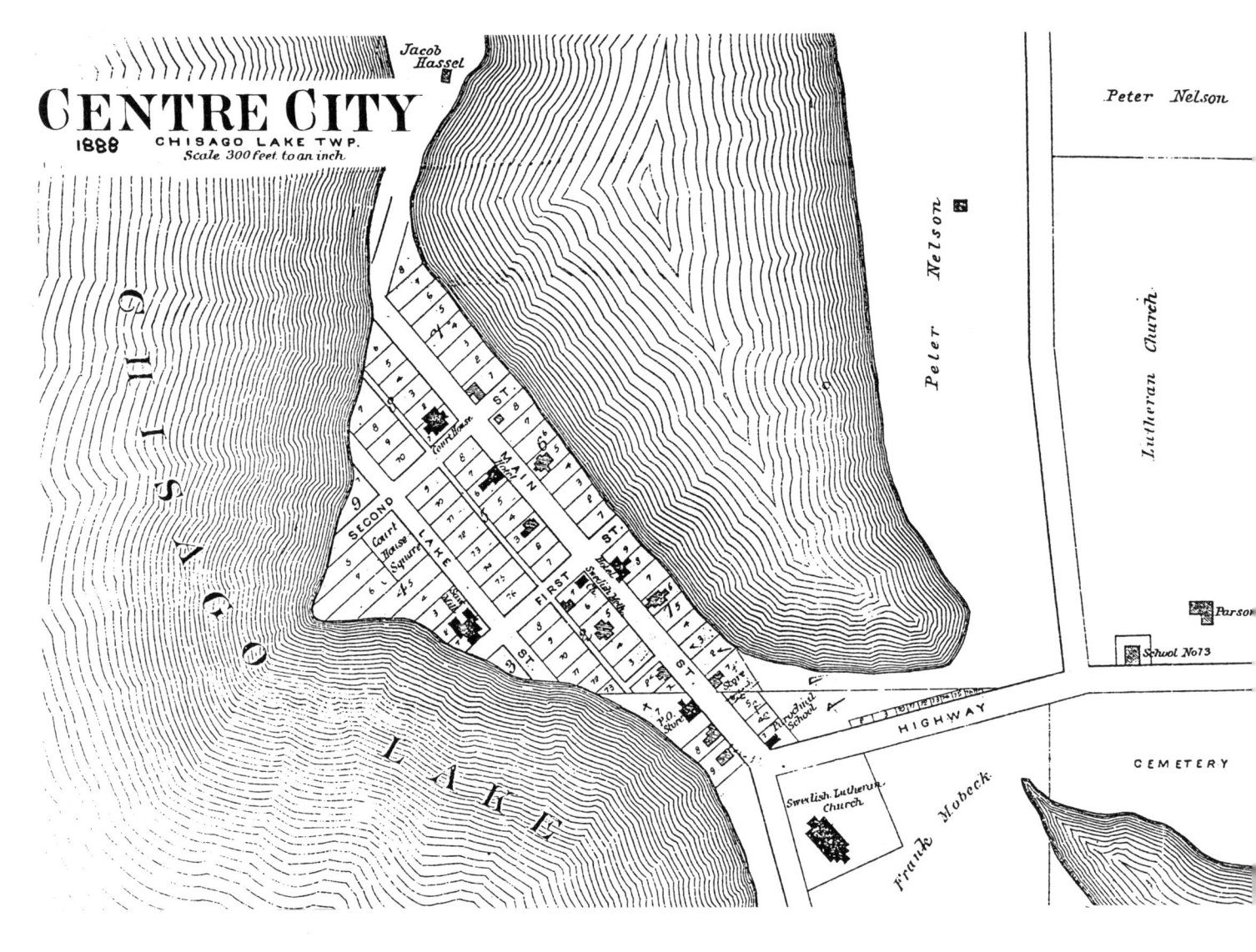

CHRONOLOGY: 1871-1930

1871   Lake Superior and Mississippi Railroad completes track from St. Paul to Duluth running along the western edge of the county.

1880   Second big wave of settlers over next three years. Railroad completed from Wyoming to Taylors Falls, running through Chisago City, Lindstrom and Center City. New housing, business begins to shift south on Center City peninsula towards the railroad station. Lindstrom booms.

1890   Spurred by the railroad and the abundance of good fishing lakes, resorts boom.

1900   Soil begins to wear out. Farming is diversified. Dairy farming increases with creameries springing up all over the county.

1903   *Center City Press* published on November 5, 1903, one of the first Swedish language newspapers in the village. Controversy erupts over secret societies and use of the English language in church, which splits congregation at Lutheran church in Center City. Many leave church, establish English speaking Trinity Lutheran church in Lindstrom.

1912   Electricity comes to Center City.

1914   Last log drive on the St. Croix.

1917- World War I. Naval militia unit from Lindstrom
1918   is first in country called to serve.

1930   After the war, economic depression and drought bring lakes area resort era to a close.

County Officials.

49 Center City

CENTER CITY: FROM FARM CENTER TO RESORT AREA
(1880-1930)

Farming was still strong as the decade of the 1890's opened. The siting of the railroad about one-half mile to the south of the church motivated the businesses in Center City to move to what is now known as Lower Town, closer to the depot. Trains heavily laden with potatoes chugged to markets in the south. A starch factory was built in Center City. One year a thriving industry sprang up in Lindstrom around pumpkins, someone having discovered that pumpkin syrup tasted good on pancakes. Boxcars loaded with bottles of the new syrup found their ways to distant markets. Then one day the syrup began to return to the area. Without preservatives it had spoiled and exploded on store shelves. For a long time, older residents recall, wild pumpkins grew each summer on the abandoned pumpkin factory property east of the present-day Super Valu store.

The depot siting in Center City also encouraged the development of the peninsula south of the church which resulted in the construction of houses in the Historic District. With the coming of the railroad, the lakes also became a popular recreation area for people from the Twin Cities, Chicago, and beyond. Hotels sprang up in every town, and the packed trains rolled in three times a day spilling vacationers out into the sunny summer air of Chisago Lakes.

The resort businesses tried to hang on after World War One, but economic hard times hit hard at recreation areas. As if that were not bad enough, by 1930 the lakes were almost dry from a long drought which saw farmers plant crops in the lake beds and residents of Lindstrom walk across the dry bed of North Center Lake to the church in Center City. What remained of the resort boom ended in the Great Depression.

The trains stopped running to the area in 1948. The Lindstrom depot is gone, the one in Taylors Falls has been converted to a community center, and the Center City depot has become a bar-restaurant. The popular Dahl House Hotel in Chisago City burned down years ago, and most of the other hotel buildings, too, are gone, except for the Park Island Hotel on Highway 8 in Center City which is now a residential home. A few bed-and-breakfast houses can be found, but the only legacy of the resort era in the lakes area is the lone motel on Highway 8 in Lindstrom.

Karl Oskar and Kristina.

Fisherman still visit the area, but now they drive up in their own cars, stay only for the day and usually bring their lunches and launch their own boats. In the winter time, their private ice-fishing houses cluster on the frozen lakes.

Some descendents of the early settlers still farm, six generations later, on the same land. Unlike the feedlot farms found farther south in the state where cows stand in stanchions being fattened for the market, cows here roam freely on the green, summer pastures. One-third of area residents now commute the fifty miles to the Twin Cities for work, but the hum of cars on the blacktop roads cutting through the rolling hills and lakes seems muted here, and the Swedish influence remains strong, seen in the preponderance of blond, blue-eyed people on the streets, heard in brogue coming from the back of the Swedish Inn every weekday morning at about nine o'clock, found in the variety of ethnic foods displayed in local markets, and built into the many historic houses and buildings that still stand.

The Andersson party is long gone, but their legacy lives on in many ways, perhaps symbolized best in the dark statues of Karl Oskar and Kristina that stand high on a pedestal at the foot of main street in Lindstrom. Karl Oskar stares straight ahead, searching for new lands, while his wife Kristina turns, looking backward over her shoulder towards the old country she left behind and her roots. They are not strangers to the community their real-life counterparts, the Anderssons, founded, a community which, though it has witnessed many changes in its first 140 years, has managed to hang on to its Swedish heritage. Were they somehow to return, there is much that Karl Oskar and Kristina—or, rather Per and Carin—would find familiar here.

**Center City: From Farm Center to Resort Area
(1880-1930)**

Upper Town

*Looking south from the courthouse on
Main Street.
1900*

*Looking east from the belltower. In the
foreground are horsebarns where
parishoners stalled their horses on
Sunday.*

*Past the cemetery down the road on the
right can be seen the brick elementary
school. The road closely parallels the
original road to Taylors Falls.*

53   Center City: Upper Town

Old Main Street looking north from the church belltower 1901.

The courthouse immediately after completion in 1876. It is on the National Register of Historic Sites and is the oldest frame courthouse in use in Minnesota.

Center City: Upper Town 54

John Fredell

Fredell store is reputed to have sold the first ice cream cones in the state. circa 1904.

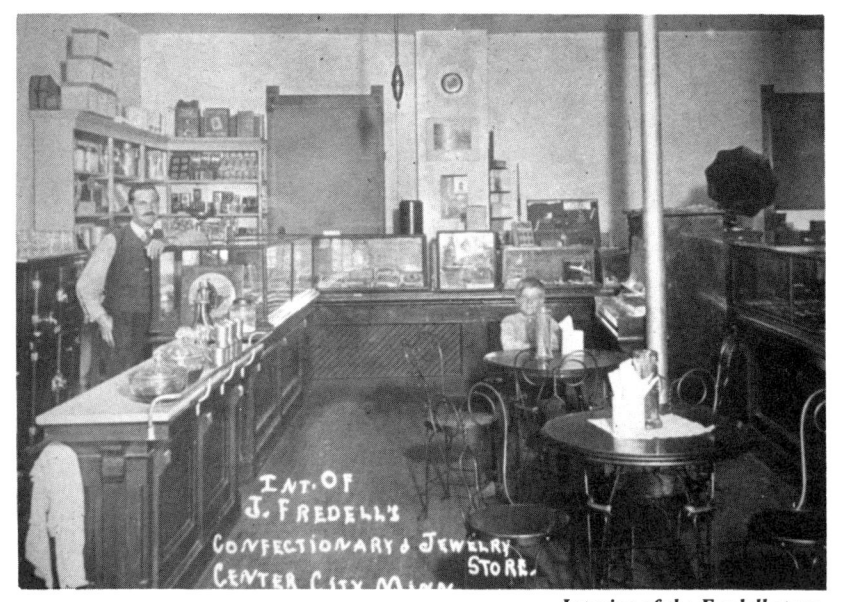

Interior of the Fredell store.

Boardwalk.

Gravestones lined Main Street in front of Westlund Monument Works.

57 Center City: Upper Town

Ad for Westlund Monument Works.

The railroad bridge separated the lake into North and South Center Lakes. People still fish along the present Highway 8 bridge.

Like ghosts from the past, members of the bicycle club stare out from 1904.

59   Center City: Upper Town

Residents gather after a fire destroyed the chapel in the early 1900's.

*Making a delivery.
circa 1909*

Center City: Upper Town 60

*The old railroad bridge entering
    Lindstrom from the west.
Painting by Carl Henrikson, Jr.*

**Taken shortly after the railroad came
through in 1880, this photo shows the
area which became the center of the
present Center City business district.**

61   Center City: Lower Town

**Center City: From Farm Center to Resort Area
(1880-1930)**

Lower Town

A shadow from the past, the roofline of the fallen livery stable on Main Street in Lower Town remains outlined on the brick wall of the town's automobile dealer.

The area in the 1890's showing the Andrews-Carlson lumber yard. The company became Interstate Lumber. Vilhelm "Willy" Carlson and his son Axel built many of the houses in the Historic District and crafted much of the fine woodwork in the Lutheran church.

63   Center City: Lower Town

Alvira "Alphie" Dahl (Johnson), the town's first telephone operator, at the switchboard in the Jirik house on Summit Avenue where Mary Andrews also first had her millinery store.

"Model T Day" drew everybody to town with their cars.

Thought to be the first automobile in town.

65   Center City: Lower Town

The newly finished Realty Building housed a theatre on the second floor. 1913

Center City-Lindstrom consolidated high school, built in 1916, had three signs on it: one faced Lindstrom with that name on it, one faced Center City with that town's name on it, and the third was on the front of the school. It simply said "High School". Not only in matters of religion were the towns of different minds.

Center City: Lower Town 66

Interior of the Axel Carlson Hardware store, 1912. It is now apartments and the drugstore.

Center City: From Farm Center to Resort Era
(1880-1930)

The Resort Era

A group of boaters on North Lindstrom Lake. Smith-Messin collection.

Park Island Hotel in Center City was built by Willy Carlson in 1893. Old-timers recall the crowded weekend trains pulling into the depot with men from St. Paul jumping off the still-moving cars to race across the bridge to the hotel so that they could ensure a fishing boat for the weekend. circa 1907.

Peninsula Hotel in Lindstrom. By this time, Daniel Lindstrom's farm had become a city bearing his name and was a popular resort area for people from throughout the middlewest.

Center City: The Resort Era 70

Playing croquet at the popular Dahl House resort in Chisago City at the turn of the century.

A group of Center City ladies try their luck. 1915.

Center City: The Resort Era 72

Recruits march along Summit Avenue to the courthouse. World War 1 marked the beginning of the end for the resort boom in the area.

A SELECTED BIBLIOGRAPHY

The following resources were especially helpful in preparing this book:

Dunn, James Taylor, *Marine-on-St. Croix: from Lumber Village to Summer Haven, 1838-1968.* Marine Historical Society.

——————, *The St. Croix River: Midwest Border River,* Holt, Rinehart Winston.

Johnson, Emeroy, *Chisago Lake Evangelical Lutheran Church, Center City.*

——————, *Early Life of Eric Norelius, 1838-1862,* Augustana Book Concern.

Minnesskrift, Illustreradt Album, *Svenska Swedish Lutherska Forsamlingen Chisago Lake,* Center City, Minnesota. 1904.

Moberg, Vilhelm, *The Emigrants, Unto a Good Land, The Last Letter Home, When I was a Child.* Simon and Schuster.

Neill, Edward D., *History of Washington County and the St. Croix Valley.* North Star Publishing. 1881.

Norelius, Eric, *The Pioneer Swedish Settlements and Swedish Lutheran Church in America, 1845-1860.* Augusta Historical Society.

——————, *Vasa Illustrata.*

Ostergren, Robert, "Cultural Homogeneity and Population Stability among Swedish Immigrants in Chisago County," *Minnesota History,* Fall, 1973.

Rosenfelt, Willard E., edit., *Washington, A History of the County,* Croixside Press.

Runblom and Norman, edit., *From Sweden to America: A History of the Migration,* University of Minnesota, Minneapolis.

Singley, Grover, *Tracing Minnesota's Old Government Roads,* Minnesota Historical Society.

Strand, A.E., *History of the Swedish Americans,* Vol. I and II. Lewis Publishing Co.

Guide to Historic Sites in Southern Chisago County

TURN OF THE CENTURY CENTER CITY:
A WALKING TOUR

The village of Center City was platted on the site of Upper Town in 1857 by proprietor Anders Svensson. As platted, the town ran north-south on the peninsula from about one block north of the courthouse to present Highway 82. The church stood across the street from the southern boundary just outside the city limits. Franz "Frank" Mobeck was in the area by 1853 and purchased the land on the peninsula south of the southern boundary in 1854. Part of his property was sold to provide land for the present Lutheran church and cemetery. Later he sold land to the railroad for a depot. Mobeck farmed and raised sheep on the peninsula. His windmill stood about where the present water tower now stands.

Summit Avenue stretches one-quarter mile north-south between Upper and Lower Towns. The completion of the railroad line through Center City to Taylors Falls in 1880 precipitated the eventual move of most businesses to Lower Town. Between the two business sections almost two dozen large houses line the crest overlooking North Center Lake, many built by resident master-carpenter Vilhelm "Willy" Carlson and his son Axel in the early 1900's. These houses were residences for tradesmen, professionals, politicians and retired farmers. A walk along Summit Avenue reveals Center City to have been a prosperous, self-sufficient village. The two-blocks of residences overlooking the lake along Summit Avenue have been designated a National Historic District, an honor which has inspired many residents to restore their houses to their turn-of-the-century elegance.

Along the dirt surface of Summit Avenue rumbled the wagons carrying marble and granite for the Westlund Monument Works from the depot to the shop in Upper Town. Westlund was a descendent of Anders Svensson, the only one of the original party of founders who had stayed in Center City. Perhaps some of his ancestors' stubbornness wore off on him for Westlund was the only businessman who did not relocate in Lower Town with the coming of the railroad.

Residents working in Lower Town seemed to climb into the clouds as they walked home to their houses on the hill. The first motor cars raised dust on the same road that in 1917 resonated to the military tred of soldiers marching off to World War 1 from the courthouse to the depot. Today Summit Avenue, also known as County Highway 9, leads travelers to the church, courthouse, and summer cabins.

Modern day vistors will enjoy the beautiful walk from Lower Town through the Historic District to Upper Town where they may visit the church archives, the old cemetery, and walk past the two blocks of red-brick-faced buildings to the oldest frame courthouse still in use in Minnesota. It and the church are both on the National Register of Historic Places.

TURN OF THE CENTURY CENTER CITY: A WALKING TOUR

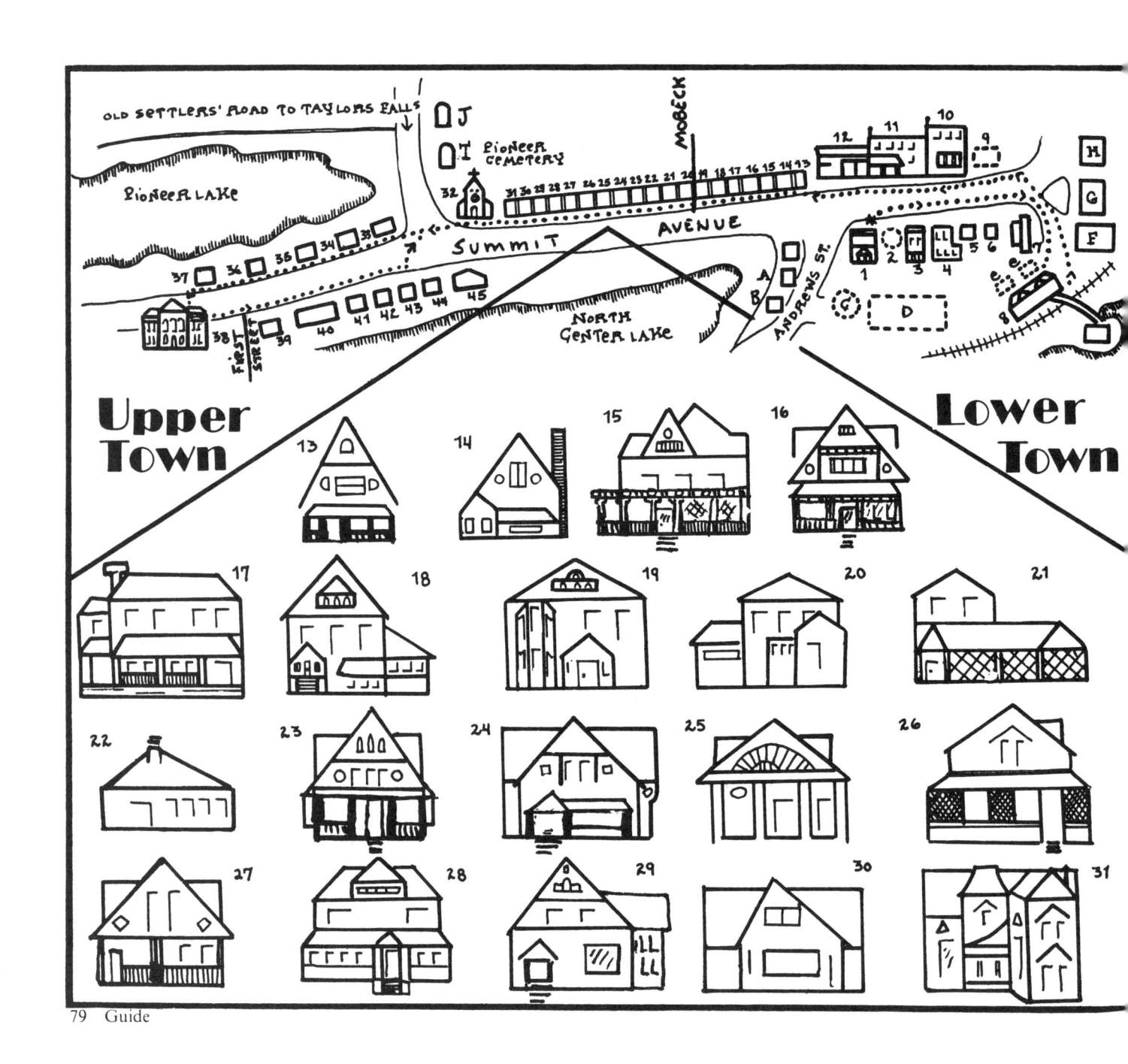

It is a .7 mile walk from the bank in Lower Town (start) to Church (finish). Side trips in Lower Town: area behind bank included a Blacksmith shop **(A)**, Sawmill **(B)**, Lumber Mill **(C)**, Lumber Shed **(D)**, Coal Sheds **(E)**, Feed Mill **(F)**, Potato Warehouses **(G)**, Section Foreman's House **(H)**; Historic walk up Summit to Upper Town; a short walk down the road to the Cemetery will enable one to visit an old settler's grave and the resting places of those who built Center City **(I)**, and the monument to Per Berg's Loge **(J)**, where the first Lutheran Church meetings were held in 1854.

---

1. BANK	• IN 1915. J. ED MELIN, BANKER
2. (BAND STAND)	• NO LONGER HERE.
3. FREDELL JEWELRY & CONFECTIONARY	• BUILT IN 1909 TO REPLACE WOODEN BLDG. LOST IN FIRE IN UPPER TOWN.
4. BUTCHER SHOP	• J.E. GOSLIN, PROPRIETOR, LIVED IN HOUSE **(24)**.
5. MILLINERY SHOP	• MARY ANDREWS, PROP.
6. PRINT SHOP/ NEWSPAPER	• EDITED BY WILLIAMS,
7. LAKE AND BURNS	• GEN'L MERCHANDISE
8. NP DEPOT	• BUILT IN 1881. THE COMING OF THE RAILROAD BROUGHT UPPER TOWN MERCHANTS TO LOWER TOWN BY THE EARLY 1900's, AND HELPED EVENTUALLY CHANGE CENTER CITY FROM A FARMING TO A RESORT COMMUNITY. VACATIONERS COULD WALK ACROSS A BRIDGE FROM THE DEPOT TO PARK ISLAND HOTEL TO THE SOUTH OWNED BY ALFRED JONASON.
9. (LIVERY STABLE)	• BETWEEN THE NOW DEFUNCT LIVERY STABLE AND LORENS; THE VILLAGE HEARSE WAS STORED HERE
10. AUTO AND IMPLEMENT DEALER	• F.G. LORENS, PROPRIETOR.

Mr. and Mrs. J.E. Melin of Center City, circa 1910.

11. REALTY BUILDING	• BUILT IN 1913, THIS BUILDING HOUSED UPSTAIRS A COMBINATION THEATER AND DANCE HALL, AND A DOCTOR'S AND DENTIST'S OFFICES. DOWN STAIRS WAS A SHOE STORE, DRUG STORE, BARBER SHOP, POST OFFICE, AND ELECTRIC STORE
12. HARDWARE STORE	• AXEL CARLSON, SON OF WILLIAM, RAN A COMBINATION STORE. THE TIN SHOP PRODUCED MOST OF THE ROOFTOP CHIMNEY LADDERS SEEN IN TOWN.

SUMMIT AVENUE HISTORIC DISTRICT
HOUSES: EARLY OWNERS & RESIDENTS

13. A.B. HOLM	• PLUMBER, WELL DIGGER.
14. WAHLSTROM	• RAILROAD SECTION FOREMAN
15. VILHELM "WILLY" CARLSON	• MASTER CARPENTER, CABINET MAKER.
16. ALFRED BERNADOTTE SLATTENGREN	• COUNTY AUDITOR
17. WILLIAM LORENS	• HOUSE LATER LIVED IN BY MARY ANDREWS
18. DR. GUNZ	• BUILT BY MARY ANDREWS FOR DR. GUNZ, M.D. WHOSE OFFICE WAS ABOVE THE DRUG STORE IN UPPER TOWN.
19. VICTOR L. JOHNSON	• BANKER, STATE SENATOR
20. JUDGE ALFRED STOHLBERG	•
21. WESTLUND	• THIS BUILDING WAS MOVED BY WESTLUND FROM UPPER TOWN. IT HOUSED A STORE, THE FIRST TELEPHONE COMPANY, AND LIVING QUARTERS.
22. AGDA WENNERBERG	• A RELATIVELY NEW STRUCTURE.
23. JAMES E. MELIN	• BANKER
24. GOSLIN	• BUTCHER
25. MARY ANDREWS	• PROPRIETOR, MILLINERY STORE
26. FRED BENSON	• RAN SAWMILL WHICH BURNED IN 1914
27. JOHN HOLTMAN	• WORKED IN LUMBER CAMPS

The house Willy Carlson built for himself. Willy lived in a small house to the rear of this while building many of the other homes in the District.

28. ELOF PETERSON	• WITH BROTHER SOLOMON RAN GEN'L MDSE. STORE IN UPPER TOWN. THIS HOUSE WAS MOVED FROM FRANCONIA.
29. SOLOMON PETERSON	• RAN GEN'L MERCHANDISE STORE.
30. V.L. JOHNSON	• LIVED HERE WHILE LARGER HOUSE **(19)** WAS BEING BUILT
31. FRANK G. LORENS	• AUTO, IMPLEMENT DEALER. THIS HOUSE REMAINS IN THE FAMILY
32. CHISAGO LAKE LUTHERAN CHURCH	• OLDEST LUTHERAN CHURCH IN AREA, THE CHURCH KARL OSKAR HELPED BUILD. VISIT THE CHURCH ARCHIVES ON THE LOWER FLOOR AND MARVEL AT THE "LARGEST RURAL CHURCH IN AMERICA." WILLY CARLSON DID MUCH OF THE WOODWORK HERE.
33. (CHAPEL)	• BURNED
34. (POST OFFICE) NO LONGER HERE	• FRANK MOBECK USED TO WALK HOME ACROSS THE SWAMP FROM HERE
35. WESTLUND MONUMENT	• ON OPPOSITE SIDES OF THE STREET, WESTLUND MONUMENT HAD GRANITE AND MARBLE WORKS.

The Lorens-Andrews house in the Historic District. In the group on the porch in striped shirts holding tools are Willy and Axel Carlson, who built many houses in the District.

The Lorens Johnson house is one of the oldest in the District. It has housed members of the same family for over 100 years.

36.	(HOTEL)	• ON THE SITE OF THIS HOUSE ONCE SAT A HOTEL AND RESTAURANT
37.	ELOF PETERSON	• MERCHANT MOVED PART OF HIS STORE TO THIS SITE WHICH IS NOW A PRIVATE RESIDENCE.
38.	COUNTY COURTHOUSE	• HERE ARE HOUSED MANY OF THE IMMIGRANT PAPERS. HERE TOOK PLACE THE ONLY EXECUTION IN COUNTY HISTORY.
39.	METHODIST CHURCH	• NOW COVERED WITH ALUMINUM SIDING, THE OLD LOG STRUCTURE STILL EXISTS BENEATH.
40.	WESTLUND MONUMENT	• RESISTED MOVING TO LOWER TOWN WHEN OTHER MERCHANTS DID. NOW THE COUNTY SHERIFF'S DEPT. AND JAIL.
41.	SITE OF GENERAL STORE	• BURNED
42.	SITE OF FREDELL JEWELRY, CONFECT.	• BURNED WHEN COBBLER NEXT DOOR KICKED OVER LANTERN.
43.	TELEPHONE CO.	• BUILT IN 1903.
44.	BANK	• BUILT IN 1903.
45.	DRUG STORE	• HERBERT SLATTENGREN, PROP.; DR. GUNZ HAD OFFICES UPSTAIRS

Part of the National Historic District.

83   Guide

Auto/Biking Guide to Historic Sites in Southern Chisago County
(No site is more than fifteen minutes by car from Center City)

Taylors Falls 85
Franconia Landing 87
Lindstrom/Scandia/
    Chisago City 89

TAYLORS FALLS

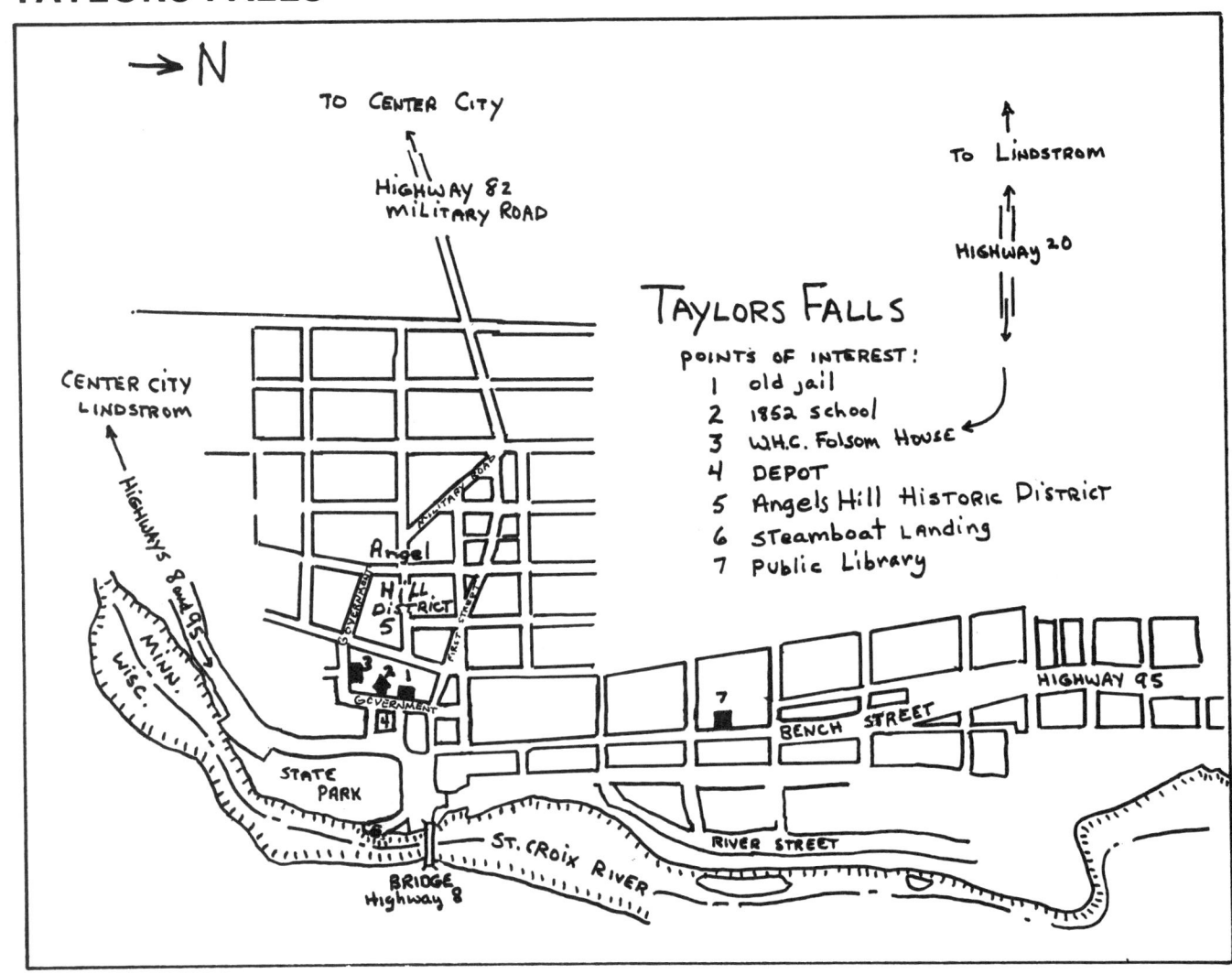

Taylors Falls Points of Interest:
1. old jail
2. 1852 school
3. W.H.C. Folsom House
4. Depot
5. Angels Hill Historic District
6. Steamboat Landing
7. Public Library

Tour A: **Taylors Falls:** There are three routes from Center City to Taylors Falls. Unless you are in a hurry, avoid Highway 8, the busiest, and take either:

1- Highway 82 past the church and cemetery on a direct line east to Taylors Falls. Though this approximates the pioneer trail, it has several miles of gravel, which may be hard on bikers. More can be seen on

2- Highway 9, north from church, to Highway 12; turn right on 12 and drive north past the Little Lake area of settlement and the Furuby school, about 2½ miles north on the right, one of the few surviving old schools; turn right on Highway 20 and proceed east to Taylors Falls. You'll pass the Yesterfarm Museum, filled with antiques and a complete log cabin; the last surviving milepost on the left at Red Wing Avenue; and drive through the Angel Hill District (NR)* in Taylors Falls with its collection of historic houses including the W.H.C. Folsom House (NR), a restored 1852 one-room schoolhouse, and renovated jail. About eleven miles. Interstate Park offers camping on both sides of the river.

*NR indicates sites now in The National Register of Historic Sites)

WHC Folsom House in Taylors Falls. Folsom was a lumberman, state legislator and amateur historian. The house, built in 1854, is in the historic Angels Hill District.

The library is on the National Register of Historic Places and is still in regular use.

Guide 86

FRANCONIA LANDING

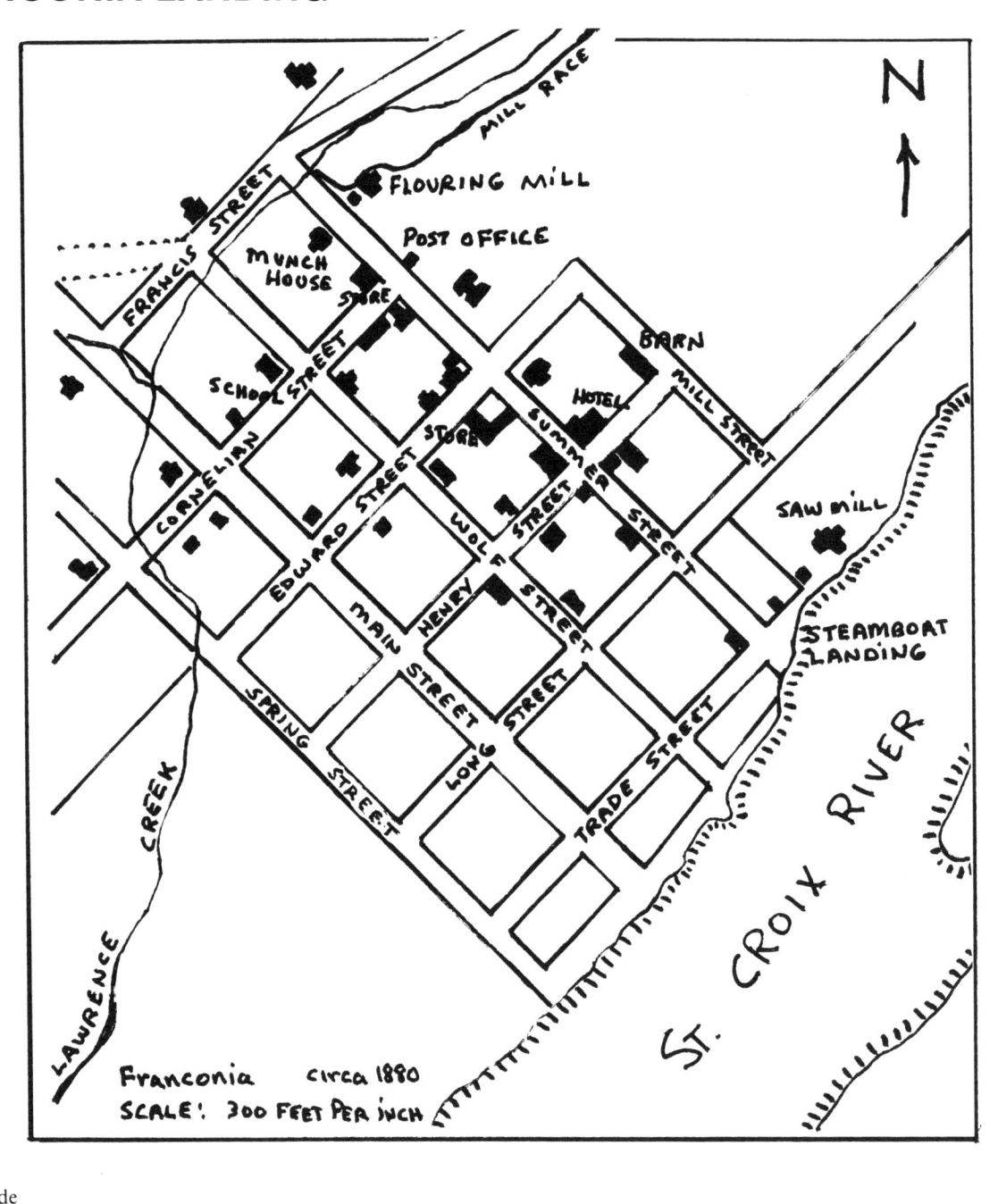

Franconia circa 1880
SCALE: 300 FEET PER INCH

Tour B: **Franconia Landing:** south of Taylors Falls on Highway 95, then one-quarter mile east on Franconia Trail. Includes landing where steamboats dropped off many immigrants, mill foundation, Munch House (NR). About five miles south of Taylors Falls.

Grist Mill, circa 1880. It stood across Summer Street (now the road to the river landing) from the Munch House.

The Munch House in Franconia was the pride of the village when it was built. Today it is on the National Register and remains a private home.

The Post Office in Franconia stood where the pioneer monument now stands.

LINDSTROM/SCANDIA/CHISAGO CITY

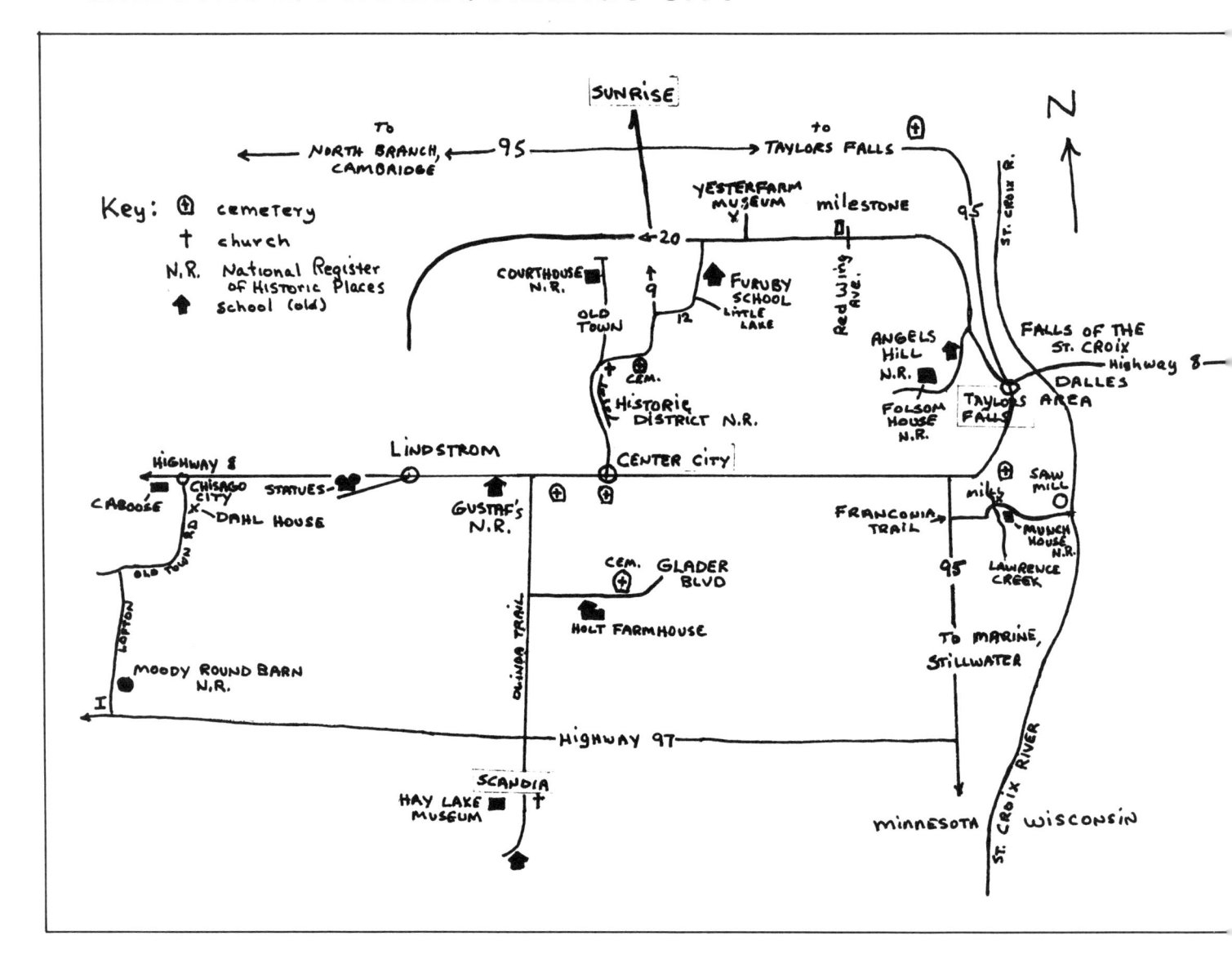

Key:
- ⊕ cemetery
- † church
- N.R. National Register of Historic Places
- ⬆ school (old)

Tour C: **Lindstrom:** One mile west of Center City on Highway 8. You'll pass the Gustaf Anderson House (NR), now a quality gift shop, and the statues of Karl Oskar and Kristina. Ethnic food is to be found at the Swedish Inn and Community Market on Highway 8. One mile back east on Highway 8 is Highway 25 (Olinda Trail). Turn south to Glader Boulevard, about two miles. Turn left on that gravel road. This takes the visitor past the Holt farmhouse on the right to a picturesque cemetery on the left overlooking South Center Lake. Return to Olinda Trail.

Tour D: **Scandia, Chisago City:** Go south from Glader Boulevard on Olinda Trail about eleven miles to Scandia. In Scandia are the Hay Lake Museum, early settler marker 1½ miles south and the Elim Lutheran church. From Scandia take Highway 52—stop sign at church intersection—northwest (left) ¼ mile to 97; turn left again and proceed 3½ miles west to county #1 (Lofton Avenue); turn right (north) on #1; three miles ahead on right you'll see Moody Round Barn (NR); continue seven miles north to Chisago City; there you'll pass the brick entrance to former Dahl's House resort on right in town; located on Highway 8 one block left is caboose #7, part of the train which brought emigrants north from 1880-1948.

Gustaf Anderson House is now a quality gift shop.

The Holt Farmhouse. When Vilhelm Moberg saw it, he remarked, "That's where Karl Oskar is going to die. Upstairs in that house."

Glader cemetery, one of the oldest in the area, was nearly abandoned and forgotten until local history enthusiasts rallied forces to restore it.

91 Guide

*Gammelgården
Farmhouse Museum*

Moody Round Barn is on the National Register of Historic Places.

Caboose #7 is a reminder of the trains that three times daily delivered loads of summer vacationers to the Chisago Lakes area. It made its last run in 1948.

Following the Moberg Trail

1988 was designated "New Sweden '88" by President Ronald Reagan in honor of the 350 years that Swedes had lived in America. Though the first Swedish settlers in America built Fort Christina in the Delaware Valley in 1638, it was not until 1851 that the first permanent Swedish settlement in Minnesota took place along the shores of the big lake at what is now Center City.

"On the 18th of July, 1850, we put our little emigrant trunk in father's old cart, and with many tears and the breaking of tender heart-strings we bade farewell to our brothers and sisters. Mother went with us as far as to the churchyard, so that she could say that she had followed us to the grave." So wrote Erik Norelius in 1916, recalling his journey almost seventy years earlier from Sweden to America, a journey that was to profoundly affect not only his own life but the lives of countless Swedes for generations to come.

In the last half of the nineteenth century one-quarter of Sweden's population emigrated to America. Norelius' group had been among the first to leave. 100 years later, Vilhelm Moberg used Norelius' party as the basis for his series of novels on Swedish emigration to America. Moberg's books and the subsequent films *The Emigrants* and *The New Land* lifted the historical activities of these Swedish settlers to mythic heights so that they have come to symbolize all Swedes who journeyed from the homeland to America.

The influence of Moberg's work can be seen in the dark, stocky figures that stand today overlooking the main street of Lindstrom. The statues gazing down on the present day goings-on are representations not of the historical Swedes who settled the area, but of Karl Oskar and Kristina Nilsson, the main characters of Moberg's novels. Such is the power of Moberg's story that a few years ago a visiting Swede stepped off a tour bus at the old cemetery in Center City cradling a bouquet of roses to lay at the grave of Kristina only to remember — or discover — that Kristina existed only between the pages of a book.

Karl-Werner Pettersson, a pilot for a Swedish airline, has made — at last count — almost fifty visits to the Chisago Lakes area, many as a guide to Swedish tourists following what has come to be known to visiting Swedes as the Moberg Trail. The summer of 1988 alone saw seventy-seven chartered busloads of Swedish tourists visit the Chisago Lakes and Taylors Falls area. In 1990, at the request of the county historical society and in recognition of the many pilgrims who travel over it, county commissioners designated Highway 8 as the *Moberg Trail*.

Vilhelm Moberg in the Chisago Lakes Area

Moberg resided in the Chisago Lakes area in 1948, gathering background information for the novels he was to write over the next ten years. Residents of the area remember him bicycling along gravel roads from Chisago City to Lindstrom and Shafer or lurking about Glader cemetery late at night reading gravestones with a flashlight. Moberg must have felt at home during his stay in the area, for the legacy of the Swedish settlers who came to the wilderness of the Minnesota Territory can be seen today in the thousands of blond, blue-eyed people bearing Swedish names who live in the area; tasted in the ethnic food found in many area stores and restaurants; heard in the Swedish brogue still spoken; and experienced by walking down the village streets and noting the Swedish architecture of many of its houses and buildings.

I'd read Moberg's novels before moving to Center City some dozen or so years ago and had found them compelling. His stories, and the fact that my paternal grandmother had been raised on a farm somewhere between Almelund and Taylors Falls, had drawn me into an investigation of the stories about the area's settlement. Many stories contained speculations about the real identities of Karl Oskar and Kristina. More than a few current residents were convinced that Moberg had written his novels about their grand-or great-grandparents.

The stories were intriguing, but perhaps the most important piece of evidence for solving the mystery of who the real Karl Oskar was came from reading Emeroy Johnson's translations of the memoirs of Erik Norelius, published in 1934. Johnson, a native of Center City, had for many years been Archivist for the Augustana Synod. Since the Chisago Lake Lutheran Church had been the birthplace of the synod, his writings about the church history naturally included many details about the settlement of the Chisago Lakes area.

Erik Norelius Memoirs

In his memoirs, Erik Norelius recounted the emigration of about 100 people from and around Hassela parish in Halsingland, Sweden, following them from their departure from the home parish in the summer of 1850 to their arrival in Illinois on a snowy day in the early winter of the year. With the onset of winter, the remaining members of the party (almost half had dropped out on the journey from New York inland) settled in with Swedes who'd arrived earlier.

*Old Man of the Dalles
Photo circa 1865.*

Over the winter, the leader of the party, Per Andersson, a relatively well-off farmer from Hassela, corresponded with Erik Norberg, a former Janssonist who was wintering in the lakes area of Minnesota Territory about nine miles west of the Falls of the St. Croix. Norberg's Letters and maps apparently interested Andersson for when the ice broke up in spring his family, and those of Peter Viklund and Per Berg, headed northward towards Minnesota Territory (Erik Norelius, however, went East to Columbus, Ohio to study at a seminary. He first visited the colony in 1854). The Andersson party was joined en route in Galena by the family of Anders Svensson. The four families and Andersson's hired hand Daniel Rattig arrived at the Falls of the St. Croix on April 23, 1851, cut a trail westward some nine miles, and settled on the shores of what is today North Center Lake.

It is clear that Moberg was familiar with Norelius' memoirs. His copy of the memoirs rests today in the Emigrant House Museum in Wexio, Sweden. Underlined are specific passages relating to the journey of the Andersson party. The path taken from Sweden to the Falls of the St. Croix by Moberg's fictional party is identical to that taken by the Andersson group. Examples of other similarities between fiction and history include the following: both journeys took eleven weeks, nine died en route in both accountings, and the name of the ship traveled on the Great Lakes by both was the *Sultana*. One departure in the novels is that the original party had come from Halsingland, while Moberg had his group start their journey in Smoland, his home province.

Moberg's Uses of History and Geography: the Old Man of the Dalles

A more significant difference between fiction and fact is in Moberg's use of local geography and state history. In his novel *The Last Letter Home* he moves the "Old Man of the Dalles" from the rocky bluffs of the St. Croix River near Taylors Falls to the shores of Ki-chi-saga (North Center Lake). Moberg also transports incidents occurring during the Dakota Conflict (sometimes called the Sioux Uprising) of 1862 from the Minnesota River Valley to the vicinity of the Swedish settlement at Center city. Having the rock-cliff-face close to Karl Oskar's home serves Moberg's story well in that he makes of the "Old Man" the face of an Indian. When the Conflict goes well for the Dakota (Sioux), the rocky face of the Indian glows and the surrounding trees and grass flourish; when the tide turns and the Dakota are driven away, Karl Oskar sees the rocky face darken and crumble.

In actuality, though news of the Conflict panicked some of the Swedes in the colony to the point where a cannon was brought to the settlement from Ft. Snelling, no skirmishes occurred locally. Events of this biggest battle between Indians and whites in American history took place some hundred miles to the south and west along the Minnesota River moving generally from the ferry at Redwood towards Ft. Snelling. In fact, several of the local settlers reported that they could not have made it through those first Minnesota winters without the help of the Indians in the area who brought food to their cabins, in some instances on a weekly basis.

Moberg's Characters: Fiction and Fact

Moberg's main fictional characters also reveal a mixture of history and fiction. Readers of the saga will recall that Kristina was devoutly religious, appealing to Karl Oskar to stay out of the Civil War for God's sake, and ignored the doctor's warning that her next pregnancy might lead to her death. Due to an old injury to his leg, Karl Oskar failed his enlistment physical, much to Kristina's relief. Later, when Kristina invited Karl Oskar to her bed he entreated her to remember the doctor's warning, but Kristina, trusting to divine providence, prevailed and her ensuing pregnancy resulted in her death.

Karl Oskar, always skeptical of divine providence, relied not on the church but on the sweat of his own brow — perhaps reflecting Moberg's own beliefs. In this, he differs greatly from his historical counterpart, Per Andersson. Andersson has been called the first Lutheran layman in Minnesota. In the absence of a minister in the colony, he baptized the newly born and later was a founder of the Lutheran church in the colony. It was Andersson's letter to his old friend Erik Norelius that brought the young divinity student to the colony in 1854 to minister to the congregation and become the colony's first teacher that summer. Andersson was a church leader wherever he lived in Minnesota.

A curious detail about the original party of four families is that only one, that of Anders Svensson, stayed in the Chisago Lakes area. Unlike his fictional counterpart Karl Oskar Nilsson who died on the farm where he had settled, Per Andersson, the leader of the historical party, eventually settled in Cambridge, where he is buried in the Lutheran cemetery with his wife Carin. Their gravestone identifies him as the founder of the Center City colony.

In the early 1900s Per's son Daniel, like his father before him, led a group of immigrants, this time from Minnesota to California where his descendents reside today.

Though most of the original party had moved on by the early 1860s, Swedes continued to arrive in the colony in increasing numbers. In April of 1851, only sixteen Swedish settlers lived on the eastern shores of the lake, but by 1855 their number had increased to almost 500. Cholera had

Little Crow, reluctant leader of the Dakota in 1862.

taken its toll in the mid-50s and the national economic panic of 1857 temporarily slowed immigration, but Swedes continued to pour in until the area could boast that more Swedes could be found only in the homeland. Today, California makes that claim.

The record shows that Erik Norelius' mother had not "followed her sons to the grave" when they emigrated in 1950. Though she thought she would never see either Erik or Andrew again, time proved her wrong. In 1854 she arrived in America and settled on the north shore of Little Lake in the Center City settlement.

Now, almost thirty years after Moberg's death, history and fiction live side-by-side in the communities the Swedes built. Anders Svensson, his name Americanized over the years to Swanson, the lone member of the original party to live out his life in the area, is survived by a grandson, Merle Swanson, who lives in Lindstrom next to the house in which his grandparents finished out their lives. With other male descendents of Swedish settlers, Merle often spends his mornings across main street from the statues of Karl Oskar and Kristina, sipping strong Swedish coffee in the back of the Swedish Inn.